Myth

ERIN RITCH

TABLE OF CONTENTS

PART ONE

I

THE LOST WANDERER

"The rain fell heavy on his head, bleeding into his eyes. It had been pouring like that for days, wearing him down. The rain wanted to make him one of their own. To wash him away piece by piece until he belonged to them. His horse, Shilee, heaved hot, steamy air from beneath his saddle. The man paused at the cross-roads in front of him. He had to press on. He had to keep looking, keep believing. Everything depended on this. Everything."

Roland paused for effect, watching the faces of the two children in front of him. He had turned down all the lights in the living room, illuminated now only by the dramatic firelight. His grandson, Shogun, sat on the edge of his seat, eyes wide. Roland nodded and continued.

"From underneath his soaked jacket, he pulled out a crumpled piece of paper. He studied the lines on the page as he had a hundred times before. A place from a dream roughly outlined in the early morning light. His fingers had shook with adrenaline, frantic to capture every detail, great and small. When the sun finally rose, he was gone. Shilee packed and his compass in his pocket, chasing the storm in the distance. His empty house could die without him. All would be right if he found this place, he knew it to be so."

Roland paused again to catch his breath, his fist still hovering in the air. He looked down at Shogun's little friend, Madigan. She watched him darkly from beneath her halo of brown hair, her mouth poised with a question.

"Thunder rumbled in the distance then a flash of lightning!" Roland continued before Madigan could interrupt him. "The storm was growing impatient. Suddenly, the man's pocket grew very hot. He drew out his compass. It glowed and burned in his palm. The hands of the compass circled wildly, pausing, then spinning around again. Finally, it chose a direction and with a kick of his heels, he urged Shilee forward. They ran like the lightning that scorched the ground around them, electric and quick. He held the shining compass out in front of him like a torch, charging on faster and faster!"

Madigan glanced over her father, Jacob. He was watching from the side, looking amused at the old man's theatrics. The living room was warm. Too warm, almost suffocating to her. The entire floor plan of the house seemed to be centered around the wood burning stove that blazed from the heart of the room. There was a table with chairs, an orange couch, and wood chips strewn around the room for no apparent reason. Madigan crinkled her nose at the axes, saws, and ropes that were displayed across the walls. The only thing that kept the house from looking like a typical woodsman's house was the large rug that covered the polished oak floors. It looked as though a million different hands had taken years to finish it, but its rich mauve color and perfect stitches were worth the effort. The windows of the house were foggy with the collision of warm, inside air and cold, outside air.

"I'm confused. Where is he going?" Madigan whispered to Shogun.

Shogun wiped the sweat from beneath his mop of blond hair. His grandfather had stopped for a brief moment to take a quick puff of his wooden pipe, wiping away the sweat from beneath his own thick layers of gray hair.

"He doesn't know!" Shogun whispered back sharply. "Shh!"

"Without warning," Roland's voice suddenly boomed across the room. "A dark form rose from the ground ahead of him. Starting as a pool of black, it rose into the hunched form of a cloaked body. It reached into the sky with a crooked hand and turned in the man's direction. Shilee bucked and sent the man flying to the ground as the dark figure cackled away."

Shogun glanced up at his father, Paddie, as he entered the living room. He had been in the kitchen, avoiding the story he had heard a dozen times before. His face was long and quiet in the faint light, his shaggy black hair hanging into his eyes as he leaned against the wall. Shogun turned back to his grandfather. He had heard this story a dozen times, too.

"*Give me your compass,* the creature shrieked," Roland continued, raising his arms. "It was now that the man saw what this thing was – a grotesque, twisted shadow woven from the darkest magic. The creature raised its arms and the cloak began to flap in the stormy wind like giant, dark wings."

Madigan stirred in her seat. She looked down at her hands, tightly clenched in her lap. She recoiled as Roland suddenly turned around with his sword drawn.

"The man ran towards the evil demon, cutting it down with his sword. He had to protect the compass at all cost. It was his only way back to his family. The creature screamed and tumbled through the air, the sword still lodged in its cold heart." Roland turned serious. "He could have run but the man would not leave his sword. The sword of his father and his father before him. He stepped closer and placed his hand on the hilt of the weapon, carefully drawing it out of the creature."

Shogun inhaled deeply.

"With a long, ragged gasp the creature breathed again!" Roland roared, his shadow rising twice his height in the firelight. "It screamed at him and struck the man, sending him rolling across the ground, breaking the precious compass. The creature shot into the air and hovered over the man, its long mouth open in a shriek. Then it disappeared from sight."

The room was electric with tension. Roland had begun to settle down, reaching for his rocking chair and pulling it near the fire. He puffed long, thoughtful breaths, enjoying the rapture of his audience.

"The compass was broken forever. The man cried. Deep tears like none other," Roland finally whispered with his eyes closed, rocking back and forth rhythmically. "His compass laid by his side, the hand fallen limp. No prayer could fix it. No trick or tool. *But he still had his map*, he told himself. And he still had his dream."

Shogun felt his eyes begin to moisten. He wiped them quickly, thankful to be disguised in the darkness. Every time, this point in the story transported him back to that rainy plain. He imagined the helplessness of the man, the broken compass in his clenched fist. He imagined himself there, as the man, the sword dripping with rain. Roland continued to rock back and forth and puff on his pipe, making a sort of rhythmic melody of creaks and breaths.

"So the man tucked the map back in his pocket and started walking," Roland sighed, opening his eyes. "And he became known as a lost wanderer, searching for the secret to bring his family back. Everything depended on this. Everything."

The room was quiet besides the squeaking of the rocking chair and Roland's steady pipe. Shogun stared at his feet, outstretched in front of him. Madigan looked over at her father. He had been listening very intently, all amusement gone from his face. She walked over to him and wrapped her arms around his waist. His neck smelled like salt. Maybe it was sweat or maybe it was from the sea. Maybe he had absorbed so much of the ocean that now his pores began to purge it through his skin. Jacob looked down at her, a small smile pulling at his lips.

"Quite a tale, Roland," he began to laugh, running his fingers through his dark hair. "What a way to end an evening."

"That it is," Roland agreed with a nod, removing his pipe long enough to respond. "Good for you fisherfolk to hear tales like that. Gets your blood pumping like it should." He replaced his pipe and took a long drag, finally replacing his sword now that the show was over.

"I'm sure they have tales of their own," Paddie added, crossing his arms over his chest. "They don't need ours."

"I still don't understand where he was going and why it was going to bring back his dead family," Madigan whispered to herself. Her family did have tales of their own, but they made more sense than that one.

"He doesn't know, that's why it's a good story! Just leave it!" Shogun shouted as he stood up. "You don't have to understand everything!"

Madigan scoffed. The house seemed to shake from the sudden outburst, catching Roland just as he was taking an exceptionally far lean back in his rocking chair. He tumbled unceremoniously to the floor, although the pipe managed to stay locked between his teeth.

"Damn dammit, Shogun!" Roland bellowed as he struggled to his feet.

Shogun was in his bedroom with the door latched shut in an instant. Paddie shrugged and returned to the kitchen. Jacob looked around at the chaos in the woodsmen's house and smiled to himself, but Madigan caught it. She had to be quick, but she caught it. He had frozen the situation in his mind and realized he was no part of this and this was no part of him. Madigan slipped her hand into Jacob's palm because it was still small enough to do that. She was twelve and Shogun was eleven. She was still small enough to do that.

"We'll be heading home, now," Jacob announced, winking at Madigan. "As always, thank you for the hospitality. And please, try not to kill the boy."

Paddie resurfaced from the kitchen. "Good night, then," he murmured in a low, calm tone. He had a chipped white mug in his hand, steam rising like spirits from its depths. His lips were dry and cracking until he wet them with his brown tongue. His eyes were heavy as he closed them, savoring the hot drink. Madigan crinkled her nose.

The two fisherfolk were already out the door by the time Roland responded with a gruff wave of his hand. He had given up on getting Shogun to open his door and was returning to his overturned rocking chair. *That damn dammit boy.* If he hadn't been the last in the Saban line, he might've shown him what a real beating felt like. Maybe. Roland settled down in his chair and took a long inhale from his pipe. That was he sure of.

His friends laughed at him for knowing a fisherman. Of course, they all knew fisherfolk in some way, but none of his friends actually *knew* them. And this would have been the same for him, if not for the day Shogun went lost. He and Paddie had searched everywhere, on the verge of giving up. But when night had almost fallen, a young fisherfolk girl showed up at their door in her wet jeans and purple shirt. She had just pulled a headstrong yet inexperienced Shogun from a riptide. The girl was Charlotte Madigan or Madigan as everyone calls her. A girl strong enough to bear the name of her ancestors, he supposed.

There was silence in the house until Paddie screeched a chair across the floor and came to sit by the stove. He stared at the flames performing within the confines of the stove, his hands hovering in front of the radiating heat.

"What is your fascination with that story?" Paddie asked his father, examining his hands in the firelight. The light did not go near his face, only licking at the edges, testing the perimeters.

"Swords, fighting, demons, adventure. It is an old story, Shogun has loved it since a boy," Roland listed off curtly to his son. "And you. What is your distaste for it?"

Paddie's face was blank and guarded. "Dead family, brought back again?" He sat back, his arms resting on his legs. His hands and fingers were caked with dirt and sawdust.

"Hmm," Roland murmured through his pipe. "I see."

"No more of it," Paddie said, standing up from his chair. He brushed off his pants and drops of sawdust fell through the air like rain. His heavy boots stomped down the hallway and his bedroom door shut.

"That damn dammit woman," Roland sighed heavily, extinguishing his pipe. "Still a thorn in my side, even from the grave." He turned off the lights and lumbered to bed.

Shogun was listening at his door. He heard when his father went to bed, those heavy boots were unmistakable. His grandfather had more of a shuffle as his shoes scuffed across the wood floors, summoning electricity that the house loved. Shogun was prepared to feign sleep at any moment but Roland passed his grandson's room without pause. He had never been beaten, but once he had come close and close was close enough for Shogun. Once he heard his grandfather's bedroom door shut, Shogun slowly climbed onto his bed, being careful not to draw any attention to his room by triggering creaky boards.

He crept across the mattress, avoiding any loud springs, and peered out his window. First, his eyes emerged, then his nose rose to smell the dust on his windowsill, and finally his chin to rest his face against the cool glass. Shrunken Hollow Road was preparing for sleep. The trees were gathering themselves, their leaves and branches breathing the last sigh of evening. Shogun rested his head on his arm, listening. Watching. Once they were done, he laid down and tucked his arms behind his pillow, allowing his mind to wander back to that rainy plain. The man was still walking into the horizon, his sword in one hand, the broken compass in the other. He walked until Shogun fell asleep and forever after.

II

THE SAND IN THE STONES

Jacob and Madigan walked slowly down Shrunken Hollow Road, chuckling over their evening at the Saban house. The other fisherfolk didn't understand how they could be friends with those strange woodsmen with their axes and ropes. Their cut and dry philosophies, absent of much feeling or much believing. Except in their tales, Jacob mused. But Jacob and Madigan saw a strange tenderness to them, a loneliness that reminded them of the sea. And they would always be drawn to the sea no matter what.

The forest there was strong, but not so strong as to block out the sound of the ocean in the distance. Jacob hesitated and listened. He took a deep breath.

"Can we wait a minute? I want to show you something," he said quietly.

Madigan sighed loudly. She sensed where this was going. "Papa, I just want to go home! Now, really?"

"If you're worried about your mother, I'll take the fall for this one. Come on, humor me," Jacob urged.

Madigan didn't answer and let the silence do it for her. She looked at her father through the corner of her eye. It was getting very dark out, but she could still see the mountains and the rivers and the valleys on his face.

"All right, then," Jacob laughed with a shrug. He began clearing away a patch of gravel in front of him. He scooped the stones to the side, being careful to shake off any sand. "Just watch."

Jacob drew a circle in the sand with his finger. It was a perfect circle with no stops or starts, just continuous movement. He pointed at the circle and looked over at Madigan, who was watching him carefully. He knew what she was feeling. "What does this look like?"

Madigan kept her eyes on the circle, as though it would pop out of the sand and go whizzing through the air into oblivion. "A circle."

"Go a little further." He knew what she was feeling. She could try to hide it all she wanted.

"A circle. A fence? A boundary?" The circle shifted in her stare and she flinched.

"Put it all together. Sand. Circle. Sand. Circle," Jacob repeated, pointing to the objects that accompanied the words. She could try to fight it. But she wouldn't win.

Madigan envisioned the beach that was only yards away. Swelling and receding. Breathing new life and old. She saw the wind as it picked up sand and placed it somewhere else, over and over again endlessly. In her mind, she followed the wind as it twirled its fingers around some chimney smoke.

"Smoke? A fire pit? Is it a fire pit?" she exclaimed in a rushed whisper.

Jacob smiled and clapped. He reached out to hold his hands over the circle as though warming them in the invisible flames.

"Good job, Maddie! Now, what's in a fire pit?" he asked.

"Fire."

"What does fire need?"

"Wood."

"More than that. Think basics. Fire doesn't always need wood to burn, does it? Grass can burn. Coal can burn. Think about what's here right now. Right at this very moment. What do you have to make a fire?"

Madigan paused. She was getting drawn into one of her father's teachings on the elements again and she had walked right into it. He didn't do it often, but at certain times and certain places, something moved him to speak about it. She tried a few times to answer before finally gathering the courage to venture her initial thought. "Air?"

The air snapped. "Good!" Jacob shouted, startling Madigan enough to scoot a few feet away from the circle. She backed into a tree trunk and let its branches enfold her.

The circle began to pulse, glowing in the dark sand. Jacob was hunched over the fire, rubbing his hands together as though they had been cold for a very long time and finally there was warmth. The fire shot up and stretched towards the sky until the flames recognized each other and intertwined. They burned purple and blue and finally reddish orange, settling within the confines of the ring of sand. The smoke smelled bittersweet, tickling Madigan's nostrils.

Jacob wiped his hands and nodded, appearing satisfied. He watched as Madigan emerged from her hiding place. She inched forward, her gaze locked on the fire in front of her. It was small and contained, as though still discovering this brand new world. Jacob folded his hands in his lap.

"Do you think the fire is real?" Jacob asked her.

Madigan fanned her flushed face. The heat seemed to be getting more intense by the moment but she was transfixed by it.

"It won't hurt you. Watch."

Madigan gasped as her father plunged his hands into the flames. She covered her eyes, expecting to hear a scream, but she only heard the steady cracking of the fire. As she uncovered her eyes, her father's hands were still there.

"Tell me again. What's here? Just the basics," Jacob quizzed, slowly withdrawing his hands and holding them up for his daughter to inspect.

Madigan concentrated. "Sand."

Jacob nodded.

"A circle." The heat from the fire began to lessen although the flames remained the same.

"Air," she finished. Now the heat was comfortable, almost welcoming. It was just sand, a circle, and some air. She reached out and touched the floating flames, inspecting them. They were lukewarm.

Jacob was smiling. He nodded to himself as he stood up and brushed off his pants. He came to stand next to Madigan as she repeatedly thrust her hands into the fire.

"I'll explain," Jacob said, watching the thoughts flicker across his daughter's face. "When I made this, I made it with love. So you could see in the dark as we walk back home. And I didn't actually *make* the fire. I just told the sand and the circle and the air that if they came together they could make this wonderful thing. Make sense?"

The flames were beginning to explore beyond the reaches of the circle, testing the edges. Jumping up and looking around then crashing back to the ground. They would get a glimpse of what could be and that glimpse would be enough. Maybe too much. So the flames pulled back.

"I want to go home," Madigan said quietly. She kicked loose soil into the fire until it sputtered and died out. The night engulfed them now, freed from where it had been lurking around the edges of the firelight. Jacob's face fell dark.

"I don't want to learn about the elements," Madigan said with finality, meeting his gaze. "Stop trying to teach me."

Jacob looked down at the muddled circle. The last threads of smoke were twisting into the air, evaporating into the end of yet another day. He pushed his finger around in the cool soil. It was gone. Wrapping his right arm around Madigan, they continued walking back home, stepping in perfect unison. Maybe on purpose. Maybe not. Jacob sighed and looked up at the stars.

"All right, my love," he whispered. "Maybe another day."

III

THE WOODSMAN'S APPRENTICE

Of all the sounds a blade could make, the whisper as it is unsheathed was Shogun's favorite. Like an inhale it cuts through the anticipating air. Then, a strike. A split. He loved the sound as a crisp branch snapped beneath the sharp blade's wrath. It has to break. It has no other choice. The tree sighed as a branch tumbled to the forest floor. Shogun ran over and pulled it away quickly, his hands becoming wet with sap. Sticky and wonderful, the sap was heavy with the scent of a million days concentrated into one drop.

"Boy!" a voice shouted from the sky.

Shogun jumped. He was outside in his oversized red sweatshirt and his grandfather's boots, both too big for his young frame. It was very damp that day as the moisture floated aimlessly in clouds of mist, contemplating its purpose and direction.

"I'm here!" Shogun hollered back into the treetops. He wrapped the ends of his red sweatshirt sleeves around his numb fingertips. He would have loved to stand beneath the trees and look up into the tornado of falling debris, but his grandfather would never allow it. *Too dangerous*, he would say in a cloud of pipe smoke. But Shogun still wanted to see why.

"I'm coming down. Now, you watch me. It's wet out, so the trees are slick and the ropes don't like that. Are you paying attention?

Damn dammit, boy! Come closer! I'm losing my voice!" Roland's commands echoed through the trees.

Shogun obeyed his grandfather and ran across the backyard of muddy grass. The trees seemed very tall and Roland seemed very high up. Shogun guessed it would have made for a great view of the ocean, but Roland didn't care about that. He was tangled in a giant spider web of ropes and rusty hooks, suspended in the highest part of the treetops. Roland dangled in the air and knocked down the occasional cloud of dust as he bumped against the great fir tree he was tied to. Shogun pressed his palm against its bark. It was a good tree.

"You there?" Roland swung his torso around to get a better view of the ground. Shogun saw the glint of the giant sword strapped to Roland's back. It was magnificent. Shogun waved in a daze as he stared at the blade.

"Good, I'm getting hungry. Now, watch me. Just don't tell your pa," Roland grumbled, wrapping his right arm around the thick rope. It dangled from the treetops to Roland's waist, down to the excess that was neatly piled on the forest floor. The old woodsman yanked the rope hard and called out, as though his shout was a battle cry and the rope was his trusty steed. In a haze of dust and dirt and tree shavings, Roland came whizzing down the side of the tree and stopped a few feet from Shogun's shielded eyes.

"Did you see?" Roland asked breathlessly. He was getting old. A climb like that used to be of no significance to him.

Shogun pressed his lips together and shrugged. Of course he had seen, but maybe if he pretended he hadn't his grandfather would show him again.

"Ah, boy. Pay more attention," Roland grumbled. His dry, lumpy fingers fumbled with the harness around his waist. It finally released and Roland stepped out as though it was nothing. As though he hadn't just been flying. He reached his arms over his shoulders and swung the sword into the air and in a blink it landed in the firm, wet soil. "Come on, I'm making your lunch," he sighed, slapping the back of Shogun's head in his own playful way.

Shogun walked with his grandfather back towards the house, tripping as he looked over his shoulder at the upright sword. The light flashed off the blade in a dozen different directions even beneath that overcast sky. It seemed to stare back at Shogun as the blade settled into the earth, hibernating in a calm suspension until the next time Roland needed him. And it would be ready.

Inside, the house smelled like damp earth and sawdust, just as they liked it. Roland kicked off his muddy boots and Shogun did the same. With footsteps that sounded like thunder on the hardwood floors, Roland walked over to the kitchen. He sighed loudly at the way the cool floors felt beneath his hot, swollen feet and swung open the refrigerator door. It was an old refrigerator of an ivory color that was once winter white but the forest dust put a stop to that. Shogun watched from a few steps behind, his thick socks drooping down his legs and ankles to his feet. Maybe one day everything would fit. Roland and Paddie were determined to dress Shogun like that until he did. Maybe it would speed up the process.

After almost a minute of careful thought over the contents of the refrigerator, Roland decided. "Sandwiches. Ham. With mayonnaise."

"Cheese? Swiss," Shogun spoke up. He tried to make his eyes very big so the rest of his facial features would look gaunt. It worked as Roland begrudgingly tossed the pack of Swiss cheese onto the speckled blue countertops.

Shogun grinned and settled into his seat at the table. He loved the way the house felt on those days. At that time of day, when the shadows came naturally and were not thought to be strange. Time moved stealthily, disguised by the overcast skies. Shogun felt safe without even realizing it and Roland's sandwiches only made it better. He listened as his grandfather sang while he rhythmically assembled lunch. It was an old song with old words that became un-earthed from his subconscious when he didn't realize it. Roland tossed a sandwich to his grandson and Shogun pressed his fingers into the soft, white bread. He loved the way the house felt on those days.

Roland quickly assembled two more sandwiches. He placed one in his mouth and let it hang there, catching in the sharp edges of his beard stubble. He wrapped the other sandwich in a nearby rag and tied the loose ends into a knot. He rested one hip against the counter and talked through his mouthful of food. "You want to get up there, don't you?"

Shogun looked up with a start, mid-bite. He had been im-mersed in his sandwich. But now his grandfather was chewing through his words and his blue eyes were watching him very carefully. Shogun swallowed hard and could only think to nod in response. He carefully chewed the last bite of his sandwich. Ro-land seemed to think it was an adequate response since he replied back with a curt nod of his own.

"Here." Roland tossed the last sandwich at Shogun. "Take this to your pa. He can hide in the forest all day if he wants, but he's got to eat. And don't tell him I said that," Roland continued, patting the chest pockets of his shirt as he reached for his pipe. He finally found it and grinned into the pipe's wooden depths. His pipe. Like no other.

"Wait…what about the trees? Are you going to let me up there next time?" Shogun asked, his eyes darting back and forth from his grandfather to the trees outside the back door, waiting for him patiently.

It hadn't taken Roland long to light his pipe. Just a flick of a match and a gasp of oxygen and there was the flame, the pipe straddled between Roland's lips, right where it was meant to be. Roland smiled, resting his entire body against the speck-led blue countertops as he crossed his stocky arms against his chest. His shirt was an old ivory color just like the refrigerator. Maybe once it had been winter white, as well.

"You're a good boy, Shogun," Roland said with a nod of his head. He cleared his throat and thought long and hard about his next words. "It's just not time yet. One day."

Shogun sighed as he stood from the table and walked to the sliding glass door, slipping his feet into his oversized boots. There was no use trying to lace them. There was no use trying to change his grandfather's mind. *He would just have to wait for one day*, he grumbled to himself as he shut the door. Shogun walked beneath the trees. The afternoon light flickered the outlines of hundreds of leaves across his skin, over and over again with each step he took. Shogun was following the path to his father's work shed. To Paddie's secret hiding place deep in the forest where even the trees left him alone with his thoughts.

Before Shogun reached the door of the brown little shack, his nostrils instinctively twitched at the smell of fresh wood. The forest had saturated the helpless little shack and it wasn't letting go. Sap dripped down the exterior like sticky tears. Shogun hesitated before knocking. He wondered what the work shed was crying for.

"Pa?" Shogun called quietly through the closed door after his knocks went unanswered. He had learned the hard way that barging in unannounced was a problem.

"Yes," Paddie answered.

Shogun opened the shed's door and saw what he expected to see. The floor was covered with a carpet of dust and more dust hung in the air like steam in a hot sauna. Paddie sat on a stool in the corner, his back very straight and an indistinguishable chunk of wood straddled between his legs. There were indistinguishable chunks of wood everywhere. Some stood like unfinished statues. Others were mutated tables or unbalanced benches or bookcases only a few feet tall. It would have been strange to see at first, but Shogun had seen it all before.

But this time, something was different. In the center of the work shed stood the outline of a large structure, surrounded by piles of wood dust. It was just a skeleton right now, bones with no flesh. Shogun ran his hand along the smooth wood and studied the firm joints. He wondered what story this wood had to tell.

Paddie looked up. "What do you want?"

"I brought your lunch. Ham and Swiss," Shogun murmured, looking over his shoulder. To him, this was a place full of corpses. Like a graveyard of living cadavers made of wood, caught between being what they were and being something real. They looked at Shogun from the corner of their eyes, frozen in limbo.

Paddie smiled. His eyes were fixated on the piece of wood in front of him as he chopped, chipped, and sanded. "You got your grandpa to use the Swiss. Good for you. He was saving that, I think. For himself."

"For himself?" Shogun snorted. That did sound like something his grandfather would do.

"A piece of cheese helps him sleep at night," Paddie added, his voice very steady, just like the sandpaper caressing the wood.

Shogun didn't respond. He stood on one boot and scratched his supporting leg with the other boot. He tentatively held out the rag with the sandwich and Paddie took it without looking up.

"Thank you," Paddie dismissed. He dropped the sandwich to the ground.

Shogun didn't know why his father worked so hard. If he ever did finish a bench or a table or a chair it took ages to sell it, if even at all. And now he had started yet another project, one that he would likely tear down and start over again. Shogun didn't know why his grandfather never got upset. He would get mad if Shogun didn't make his bed, yet Paddie could hide in the forest all day without reprimand. He sighed and turned on his heel, quietly shutting the work shed door behind him.

IV

THE HOUSE ON THE LAST DUNE

Elise clanked the dishes together loudly. The milky water sloshed in the tin sink as her hands submerged into the suds and pulled the dishes out again, glistening and clean. She wrung the washcloth with a strong twist that seemed more than her bony hands were capable of. Her long, thin black hair was pulled back neatly and she was dressed in a thin shift, dyed to match the color of sea foam. She was barefoot, always barefoot. Just in case she needed to flee to the ocean, Madigan assumed.

Madigan was sitting at the piano in their little house by the sea. "Mama, I can't play like this. There's too much noise," she grumbled, glaring at the kitchen sink.

Elise smiled to herself. "That's what makes music different from other sounds, Charlotte. It can be heard and understood above all else."

Madigan frowned and looked down at the piano keys. Black and white, cold and lifeless. The house smelled like the ocean as the wind snuck the salty air through the open windows. Elise didn't believe in window screens so Jacob didn't put them on a single window of their two-story shanty that creaked and moaned when the big windstorms struck. The family took baths in warm salt water that Elise heated on the stove and they relieved themselves in a pit in the backyard. But Madigan thought they were civilized. Besides, the pit was covered by a small house with a little window. She made some of her best observations as she looked out that window.

The front door began to rattle. It was Madigan's favorite part of the house. Her grandfather, Charlie Madigan, said it was the first part of the house he constructed. He searched months for the perfect place to build his home, up and down the coastline. Until one day he walked atop the last dune with his heavy backpack, pushing back his cap to get a better view. That was when he finally knew he was home. He began by building the front door from driftwood and kept expanding until he built his entire house. But the door had always been and would always be first. He said it helped him remember where he'd come from.

The front door opened. Jacob walked through in a gust of wind, blowing Madigan's hair into her eyes. He walked over and ruffled her hair even more, his footsteps heavy across the wood floor. He grinned as he tugged Elise's long hair. He was happy on days like that, when all the elements were working together, telling their stories in that cool ocean breeze. Madigan sighed and replaced the cover over the piano keys. There would be no practicing when Jacob was like that.

"You should see your son out there! He's kicking up a windstorm all his own!" Jacob exclaimed breathlessly, watching his wife as she dried the clean dishes with a white towel. Elise made no visible response but she was always like that. There was always something stewing inside of her, deep beneath the surface. Just like the sea.

Jacob turned to his daughter. "Come on, Maddie. Play me a song," he asked, grinning ear to ear. He sat down on the sunken old gray couch and folded his hands in his lap.

Madigan mumbled and kicked her legs off the side of the piano bench. She learned long ago that it was pointless to try and play for her father. She was never passionate enough for him. The tempo was always too slow or she should be more hunched over the keys, hovering above the notes with anticipation. It was too much pressure.

Jacob frowned. "Well, then. We can't have gloomy feelings like that in this house. Go outside and let the sea revive your spirits!"

Madigan mumbled to herself again but obeyed, yanking open the front door and shutting it behind her. Jacob took a moment to smile at the closed door. Every time he looked at it, he recalled a memory of his father. Maybe a glance or a laugh or a pat on the shoulder. He looked over as he felt his wife's eyes on him.

Elise had folded the dishtowel and draped it over the now empty sink. She was leaning against its damp cotton, the waist of her long dress becoming wet as the towel shared its moisture. She had a way of pulling her jaw down while keeping her lips together to make her face look long and slender.

"Stop," she ordered.

Jacob stood from the couch, the weight on his shoulders suddenly more significant. He cleared his throat as he brushed off his pants, scattering sand across the quiet floor. The house had silenced itself, even shushing the rattling front door that usually reigned supreme. It wanted to hear this.

"I can't," Jacob replied, shaking his head. He shrugged his shoulders, helpless only in front of her. "I know she feels it. I know it. This is just a phase, she's scared about the thoughts she's hearing. The things she's feeling."

"That's why I've taught her music," Elise snapped and the house recoiled. She stood firm. There was not one thing of the sea that stood firm except for Elise. She took a deep breath and closed her eyes at the sound of the wind becoming tangled in the chimes. She loved Jacob's elements, they made him who he was. But music made her who she was. This was an agreement from a long time ago. And he was going back on it. "I agreed about Sara and Henry. But not Charlotte. She's different."

"Yes, she is," Jacob agreed. He set his jaw. "She's stronger than them."

"You don't know that," Elise laughed sourly.

"I do. And I can't let her keep this pent up inside. There's no pain like that. I won't stand by and allow it. I'm going to teach her. Do not stand in my way."

Jacob's voice had lowered. Even the dishes safe in the cupboards shivered at his tone, uncomfortable with the palpable tension that vibrated through the air. They settled together and swore to never come out again.

Elise did not respond. She was listening to the wind chimes, her eyes flickering back and forth. It was a message from the sea carried by the wind for her ears only.

"We will see," she sighed, turning to her husband. She brushed past him icily. There was not one thing of the sea that stood firm except for her.

Jacob listened to his wife's footsteps as she went to their bedroom and shut the door. The house let out a pent-up sigh. It was not used to the two partners fighting. Tension in that house was a strange thing, making everything else seem askew. Jacob stood at the kitchen window and listened to the wind chimes but he couldn't hear what they were saying.

Outside, the sun was shining. The Madigan house looked as though it was meant to blend in with the forest with its brown paint and green trim. But it was really just the color of sweet, salty sand wet with rain. Madigan's little sister, Sara, was sitting on the grass with her legs outstretched in front of her, cushioned by a pillow of turf. Her hair was short and made up of loose curls. She was dressed in a filthy shirt and pair of pants that had started the day off clean but now showed evidence of hard playing.

"Charlie!" Sara exclaimed, waving for her sister. Madigan waved back. She had so many nicknames she couldn't keep track. As though each name didn't quite fit so people just kept trying.

Madigan knelt by her sister. "What are you doing?"

"Nothing," Sara giggled, trying to no avail to conceal a smile. She hid a clenched fist under her legs, glancing from her sister to her hand mischievously. The wind pulled at her hair and tugged, then smoothed it down again until the tendrils fell in her eyes.

"What are you hiding?" Madigan teased. She pinched her sister's knee playfully until Sara gave in. Her fist slowly emerged from beneath her knee and Madigan carefully pried open her sister's grip.

It was an acorn. Safe and secure and unborn in the clutches of Sara's hand. Her soft skin was pink and splotchy from the forest creature's pollens. Sara was of the ocean. Forest things would have that sort of effect on her. Madigan stared down at the acorn for a few moments before looking back her sister.

Sara's angelic expression flickered but came back quickly, like a faulty circuit that refused to give up. Her features were so small and delicate and no one was sure if it was from her young age or if she was just that way. She glanced down at the acorn quickly and smiled. "Watch!"

Madigan watched. Somewhere told her what was going to happen, but she watched anyway. Sara took a deep breath. The acorn shivered as though it had felt how deep the breath was, wincing as Sara exhaled. The little acorn's top hat popped off and went rolling off the side of Sara's hand. The slick, smooth exterior of the acorn shell melted backward. Deep inside, where all the instructions for the growth of the tree were stored, a light was glowing.

Without thinking, Madigan knocked the acorn out of Sara's hand. The tiny speck of light rolled down the dune until it disappeared. Sara recoiled, her eyes tearing at the sudden loss from her hand. Her lips quivered as they turned purple with little sobs.

"Why did you do that? I was going to make it grow!" she

wailed, her voice shaking as she stood up. "I was going to make it happy!" she continued shrilly, pumping her fists as she ran around the house to the backyard, her wail trailing behind her.

Madigan groaned. She knew she shouldn't have done that. But something inside of her had reacted to that little glowing acorn, burning hot with secrets. Still, she should have just left her sister alone. The elements were welcome and asked to dinner in that house, even made a bed in the attic with the rest of the memories. She was already dreading the reprimand she would receive over this.

Down below her, Madigan's older brother, Henry, stood on the beach. He was staring up towards the house, his attention summoned by his little sister's scream. He met Madigan's gaze and flashed her a bright smile, a Jacob smile. Turning away, he outstretched his lean, long arms and his dark brown hair whipped wildly in the wind. He was practicing. He would be at this a long time, until the tide came in and insisted he call it a day.

Sunset had come very fast. The sky was filling with long, stretched clouds of pink and orange. Madigan felt strange and out of place. She had felt this way before and it was increasing in frequency. Down somewhere, there was an acorn submerged and dormant in the sand. One day, when she is very old, the tree will grow tall enough to look her in the eye every morning. And every morning will she remember this year. This month. This day.

V

THE GHOST TRAIN

Something happened to Shogun when he stretched out on the couch in the afternoon. It always got him thinking. He thought about places he wanted to go, places that weren't even real. He thought about old toys he had lost and where he had seen them last. But that afternoon, he was thinking about the trees and what was keeping him from them. And that seemed to be this *one day* that his grandfather had told him about. Keeping him stuck on the back patio, reduced to his grandfather's assistant.

"What are you thinking so hard about?"

Shogun turned his head to look at Roland. The television was muted but Shogun would have been able to hear his grandfather even if the volume was turned to full blast. He unclenched his fists and stared at Roland, who was rocking back and forth rhythmically in his chair, puffing on his pipe. It was the afternoon. There would be no more work for him that day. The house was filled with warm golden light so that everything had a golden tint whether it was gold or not. Shogun turned his head back to the ceiling.

"Nothing," he replied shortly.

Roland continued rocking, back and forth. Puff. Blow. Back and forth. Puff. Blow. That was the sequence. "You just lied to me, boy. No one ever just thinks about nothing."

"What time is it?" Shogun asked himself. It had taken him a few years, but by then he had learned how to distinguish which words from Roland were wise and which were just blather.

"Almost four o' clock," Roland replied through a puff of smoke. There was wood dust in his gray hair, sticking to his scalp like dandruff. Even he looked golden in that light. He balanced the pipe between his lips and teeth and pushed back the sleeves of his red plaid shirt. "Meeting up with a girl or somethin'?"

Shogun stood up from the couch, his green sweater gathered around the waist of his faded blue jeans. He turned off the old television set and it went to sleep with an electronic sizzle.

"None of your business," he said, the words escaping before Shogun could censor himself. He glanced at Roland and headed for the door. He walked there slowly, but he felt like running. His heels sprang at the anticipation of it.

"Eh?" Roland shouted, sitting up his chair. He leaned forward, ready to pounce. "You can't talk to me like that! Damn dammit, boy!" He coughed on a puff of smoke he had forgotten to exhale. By the time he had composed himself, Shogun was gone.

Shogun didn't stop running until he reached the end of Shrunken Hollow Road, sliding around the corner and hiding beneath an obliging fern. The front door of the Saban house was still firmly shut and didn't have any intentions of opening, it seemed. Roland wasn't following him. Shogun breathed hard. After checking once more and convincing himself that his grandfather had probably forgotten about the incident, Shogun stood up and continued down the road.

He didn't have to think about where he was walking. Shogun's body was trained, he had frequented this place so many times that sometimes his mind went there in his dreams. He walked along the old railroad tracks that hadn't felt a train for years. Or not a real train, anyway. They were rusty, covered with old moss that made its home around the edges. Soon he arrived at the entrance to their secret place, a section of the tracks completely blocked off by layers of fallen trees. A forest-made dam, so heavy and dense with years of growth that no one had bothered to clear it. So the blockade aged and took on a life of its own. Shogun looked over his shoulder and scaled the wall quickly.

Madigan was sitting with her legs outstretched across the tracks, her black boots peeking out from beneath her long skirt. She was wearing several layers of different colored sweatshirts even though it wasn't really that cold out. Shogun came to stand in front of her and she looked up from where she had been inspecting the ends of her wavy hair.

"Cutting it a bit close, don't you think?" she wondered aloud, squinting into the hazy light. She looked down at her watch and raised an eyebrow. She had been there for at least thirty minutes, well in advance of their usual meeting time. She didn't like sitting alone in the woods. There were too many smells and no air.

Shogun sat down next to her with a loud sigh. "Sorry. My grandpa."

"Makes sense, then," Madigan said with a smirk. She found the old Saban man rather entertaining with his lengthy stories and stinky pipe. He was much more interesting than Shogun's father, a grumpy figure that only lurked in the kitchen.

"He…" Shogun began, his jaw tense. "He doesn't make things easy on me, sometimes."

Madigan glanced over Shogun. Usually, it was her complaining not him. She would lament about her mother and father, both pulling at her from different directions. They thought she didn't realize it, but of course, she did. And Shogun would nod and listen, flecks of wood shavings falling from his head. His simple clothes were always covered with a fine dust, as though the trees had sprinkled pollen over him to claim Shogun as their own.

With a sudden burst, the wind charged down the tracks, sweeping any dead leaves or small branches back to the forest. There could be no debris of any kind for what was about to come. The wind pushed and shoved at the children, causing them to scramble away from the tracks. Madigan smiled at Shogun, laughing breathlessly along with him as they watched from the safety of the trees. Then they heard it. A sound that started as a horn or whistle in the distance, so faint it almost didn't happen. It echoed through the long tunnel of forest trees, stunning all life it passed on the way. Except for the ones that were watching and listening.

The ghost train whipped by them in a heartbeat, the wheels cranking and creaking in silence. Shimmering steam trailed behind the locomotive, rising like the petrichor after a rain. In the rush of wind, Madigan and Shogun could see glimpses of the passengers, the dead that were finally on their way home. Lost spirits gathered by the train, rescued from an eternity of wandering in the forest or on the beach that had no end. One day, Shogun and Madigan had stumbled upon this ghost train by accident. It took them several months to figure out why and when the train would reappear. And even then, they couldn't really explain how they knew.

The ghost train disappeared into the dam of dead trees, only the faint hiss of its engine left behind, floating into the late afternoon sky. The children breathed again, unaware they had been holding their breath. Madigan loved the thrill of the rush, the brief look into the world past her own. Shogun walked onto the tracks, staring at the wall of trunks. He was always left disappointed. He still had not seen the one person he was looking for. The spirit of his mother, the one he dreamed lived in the very highest treetops.

"Still amazing," Madigan whispered, joining him on the tracks. The forest creatures were only just starting to wrestle back to life, awakening from their temporary frozen state. She pulled up the neck on one of her sweatshirts and glanced up at the darkening sky. "I need to get home. See you tomorrow."

Shogun nodded absently. It was time for him to go home, too.

"Oh, and don't forget," Madigan added, turning a few steps down the tracks. "May Day is in a few weeks. You *can't* miss it this time."

Shogun smirked although he didn't think Madigan could see it in the fading light. May Day, the fisherfolk celebration that his family usually avoided like the plague. *Foolery on the beach*, his grandfather would say. *We don't get involved in that mystic nonsense*, his father would add. It only made Shogun more curious each time he was forced to decline an invitation.

"You don't have to do what they say, you know," Madigan said, her eyes narrowing as she sensed Shogun's hesitation. She crossed her arms, partly to stay warm and partly annoyed with the anticipated answer from Roland and Paddie. *Foolery and nonsense*, she guessed they would say.

But Shogun didn't know. The words sounded foreign to him, a thought that had literally never attempted to cross his mind. But it was the answer he needed. He was gone before Madigan could say another word, up and over the wall of rotting logs and thick terraces of moss. She heard his footsteps crunching back towards home, through the forest that was already gathering spirits for the next train.

VI

THE RED ROPE

Shogun watched from the ground. The bottoms of his boots scratched against the gray concrete patio as he shifted his weight from one leg to the other. He tried to wiggle his toes but they were all pressed tightly together within his new thick wool socks. He held his hands up to his mouth and blew hard. Even within the warmth of his palms his breath crystallized into clouds of thick air that looked like Roland's pipe smoke. Shogun looked around. The forest was very still. Watching.

It was unseasonably cold that morning. The mist was unusually dense, passing very close to Shogun's face as it inched by. Because of the fog, Roland had chosen the red rope for today's work so as to not get lost in the maze of white. Shogun watched the red rope twitch left and right as Roland moved through the treetops. He wondered if his mother's soul was somewhere in those maze of branches. All Shogun knew was that she died at their house. Maybe she reappeared in Paddie's work shed. Maybe if Paddie filled the shed with enough sawdust then it would cling to her soul and his mother would take shape again.

Shogun watched from the ground. Again. An apprenticeship that was never rewarded with pay or praise. He shuffled from one foot to the next, thinking things over and over again. Watching the treetops. The fire that had been dormant inside of him was now almost ablaze. His skin was about to turn to cinders and his teeth were about to melt in his mouth. He blew steam out into his hands again.

Roland dropped down to the ground in a cloud of soil and tree dust. He loosened the tension on the red rope but left enough for him to swing back and forth while he rested his feet. He sighed loudly and leaned his head back to check if Shogun was still there. He was still there. Standing on the gray concrete patio where there was no chance of him getting hit by a falling branch.

"Come help me out, boy," he called, stiffly removing his gloves.

Shogun reacted even before the order was uttered. Roland stepped out from his rope harness and glanced over his shoulder at the pile of wood and other debris that he had created, courtesy of an obliging tree. It was a fair amount of work for a morning that gave into the demands of the mist. He glanced upwards into the trees. He would have to wait for the mist to pass, back to the ocean where it was probably heading all along.

"Time for lunch," Roland ordered as he patted the dust from his large suede gloves and handed them to Shogun. He paused, looking his grandson in the eye. He studied his face carefully and Shogun studied his as well. Roland nodded and thrust his sword into the ground without flinching, a foot away from Shogun's hand.

"Hm," he snorted as he turned back towards the house, quietly shutting the sliding glass door behind him.

The red rope swung in the cold wind, brushing Shogun's arm where the hairs stood on end, as though summoned by electricity. *It was ready when he was.* It lived for this. It would be his beacon in the mist, its red fibers would fight for him through the darkness. Shogun reached over and touched the hilt of his grandfather's sword, carefully placed within reaching distance. The metal was freezing cold, biting to the touch. It was not for him to touch, he knew it. Slipping on his grandfather's gloves, Shogun fit the harness around his body and tucked the sword behind it, lodged against his body. He wrapped the rope around his wrist and pulled.

He blinked and was up in the trees. Shogun didn't remember how he got there but the trees nodded to him knowingly. Suddenly the forest in his backyard that he knew so well had a completely different appearance. He was close enough to the mist that he could reach his hand out and it would disappear, sucked into another realm. This truly could be where his mother's spirit lived, disguised forever in the damp maze. Breathlessly, Shogun reached out and moved to another branch and another, the red rope following close behind.

Finally, he reached the tree he had an eye on. The tree that had an eye on Shogun as well, watching as the young boy fumbled across the branches towards it. Steadying against the tree trunk, Shogun reached behind his shoulders and grasped the heavy sword. He grit his teeth as he swung down with all the strength he could muster. He exhaled as the branch cracked, tumbling down through the layers beneath it until landing in a splatter of mud. Shogun breathed hard, holding his grandfather's sword in front of his face, close enough to see the blur of a reflection. It began to shift, quivering in and out of focus until he could almost see himself.

A voice shouted from below. "Shogun!"

Shogun kept his right hand on the sword and wrapped his left arm around the red rope. Paddie was standing next to the fallen branch, gazing down at the oozing sap that was escaping from the tree's amputated arm. He looked up at Shogun, his face contorted in a scowl.

"Get down here now!" he shouted fiercely.

The sliding glass door opened and Roland exited the house to stand on the gray concrete patio. He stood there with his arms dangling at his sides like he couldn't decide where to put them. He caught a glimpse of his grandson and smirked. Looking down at his own hands, he remembered the day the ropes had been new to him, etching their names into the soft flesh of his palms.

Paddie turned to look at his father as he joined him by his side. "Lost your sword?" he asked sharply.

Roland ignored his son. "Best come down now, boy!" he shouted to Shogun, rubbing the back of his head. "The longer you stay up there, you're only going to make things worse!"

Shogun replaced the sword on his back and immediately sunk beneath its weight. He used both hands to hold onto the red rope so he could shout back with all his might. "No!"

Paddie cursed and ran his hands through his disheveled hair, walking away to pace. His back heaved up and down with each deep breath.

"I understand the rush, boy. But you don't have the training yet," Roland admonished. "You took a branch without asking, I bet. Just a quick chop here and there and think the forest won't notice, eh? Well, it does notice." His pipe had suddenly emerged. It was dangling from his lips, thin strings of smoke spiraling into the cold air.

Shogun bobbed up and down. He felt his heart beat faster and faster as this went further and further. But he couldn't back down now. "I know that! Of course, I know that!"

Roland sighed loudly and glanced over his shoulder at his son. He dropped his pipe and exclaimed as Paddie quickly approached the red rope, a small knife grasped firmly in his hand. The forest and Shogun recoiled as the two men fought, grunting as they tossed each other through the mud. Roland lost his footing and rolled to his side. Paddie placed the knife in between his teeth and reached for the red rope, wrapping it around his forearm and beginning his climb into the treetops.

"Paddie, stop! No!" Roland shouted between strained coughs. He attempted to stand up but faltered as he tried to recapture his breath.

Shogun was knocked against the tree, his head spinning as he tried to steady himself. The red rope creaked and cracked as Paddie's climb spun Shogun around in a tangled circle. He banged against the tree hard again and his grandfather's sword went crashing to the ground.

"You'll listen to me," Paddie shouted as he climbed higher, hand by hand. "One way or another."

The edges of Shogun's vision began to darken. He felt a rough hand on his arm, squeezing it so hard that Shogun thought it would burst. The trees fell into a strained silence. Watching and listening.

"Do not disobey me again," Paddie whispered into Shogun's ear. He could smell the dusty sweat on his father's skin. "Or you'll die up here like your mother."

Shogun heard the slow splitting of fibers as the knife slit through the red rope. He felt the momentary weightlessness before he crashed branch by branch down towards the ground, the tree trying its best to cushion his fall. He crumpled to the muddy forest floor, every part of his body screaming with pain.

Roland crawled over to his grandson. "Boy...boy, you alright?" he gasped, shaking Shogun's shoulders. He murmured numbly in response.

Roland looked up as Paddie descended from the trees, the knife back between his teeth. He kicked Roland's sword away from his reach, where it clattered as it slid across the gray concrete patio. Like a rag doll, Paddie picked up his limp son and dragged him through the mud back towards the house.

"You did the right thing. You did the right thing," Paddie whispered over and over, his hands shaking as he opened the sliding glass door. He paused and looked at his father. "Look what you did," Paddie shouted. "I blame you for this, old man."

Then it was quiet. Roland sat breathlessly in the mud, nursing his aching jaw. He looked around until he saw his pipe, sticking out from the mud like the branch it once was. Roland labored over to the pipe, holding it in his hand. That pipe had belonged to him for a long, long time. It had seen many things. Long sunsets. Even longer winters. Days when the darkness almost overtook the light. And now he feared it would witness the destruction of his family. He wiped the pipe off clean with his bloody fingertips and closed his eyes. And listened.

VII

THE FISHERMAN'S PLEA

Madigan sat at the piano with her hands folded together, staring at the ivory keys. They were a dull, milky color that morning as they had been every morning. It was just that this morning, Madigan had taken the time to notice. Each key was a different melody and somewhere deep inside her, she remembered how to string them together. She closed her eyes. Each day, something she knew about herself was fading away and being replaced. Maybe this was growing up. Maybe this was something else. She wondered if one day she would wake up and there would be nothing left of who she thought she was, transformed into some other person designed by the elements.

"Maddie!" Jacob shouted from outside the house.

It was morning. It was cold. The front door creaked open with a blast of air. Elise looked up from the kitchen sink. She leaned her long pale white body against the sink, her long pale dress piling on the floor. Her eyes flashed as Jacob stepped into the house. She turned back to the sink before he could notice. She must have been scrubbing a pot. Even if there wasn't a pot in the sink she could have fooled her family.

"Ready to go?" Jacob asked, standing behind his daughter.

Madigan nodded as she stood from the piano bench. She had been dressed and ready for twenty minutes. But that hadn't been what Jacob was asking. The scrubbing motion in the sink stopped. Out of the steamy water emerged Elise's glistening hands, little soap bubbles sticking to the creases between her fingers. Her hands stopped there, midair. Her eyes were wide now.

"She hasn't practiced yet today," Elise said firmly, gripping the edge of the countertop.

"No, it's alright," Madigan sighed, reaching for the door. She saw the look her mother gave her father, fierce and frantic. "I'll do it later. I promise," she added.

Jacob put a hand on his daughter's shoulder and winked at his wife. "You heard the girl. Now we have to catch the tide, my love."

They began their descent down to the beach, where Jacob's fishing boat was waiting for them. Madigan squinted up at the gray sky. It was strange that day in the way it scattered light. The sun was behind the clouds, causing the sky to glow to the point that the shadows didn't quite know where to go. The ocean swirled unhappily. It didn't like this glowing sky, either. Jacob and Madigan quickly jumped into the boat, careful to keep their clothes from getting wet. They knew if their clothes got wet and a chill set in, it was never letting go.

Once the boat was free from the beach, Madigan removed her right mitten and plunged her bare hand into the sea, touching the underside of the boat. It was slightly slimy, but if she dug her fingernails down hard enough she could feel the wood again. She removed her hand from the water and wrapped it in her bright pink scarf before her fingers were ready to re-enter the mitten again.

The boat drifted further into the sea, gently guided by the rhythmic waves. They were taken far enough from the coastline to be free but close enough to remind them that they were land dwellers, no matter how hard they wished otherwise. The fishing nets were lying motionless on the floor of the boat, waiting for their time to shine. They were supposed to be floating in a downward spiral, free in the open sea. Caught in a dance with the undercurrents that pulled them as far to the edge as their ropes would let them go. So far to the edge, they could taste the salt of freedom.

Jacob looked like a proper fisherman in his heavy gray coat that made his chest look puffier than it was. And underneath the puffy coat was a light brown fisherman-like shirt, the color of oatmeal that had been cooked too long. His boots were gray and looked as though they had been thrown on quickly since one pant leg cuff was gathered around his ankle and the other was not. He wore his usual gray fisherman's cap pulled down over just the top edges of his ears, as though that would make all the difference. His face was sharp to the touch because of his beard that wasn't an actual beard but lazy shaving. Jacob started rowing, just as steady and rhythmically as the beating waves. Forward. Up. Creak. Plunge. And after the plunge there was the sense that the oars were shivering at the sudden chill of the sea, rising above the water with a gasp. Then the process started again. Forward. Up. Creak. Plunge.

Madigan surprised herself and smiled. She liked how simple this could be. Just a set of motions. Just the rain and the memories. How many times had she sat in that boat with Jacob, the sky and sea swirling all around them. She with her own puffy coat and her bright pink scarf long enough so that Madigan could wrap herself into its warm wonderland over and over again.

"This looks like a good spot," Jacob said breathlessly, pulling the oars out of the water and balancing them on the edge of the boat.

Madigan looked around. It was a good spot, although it wasn't stumbled upon spontaneously. Jacob had probably scouted for weeks and spent yesterday sitting alone in the boat over that very spot. He always asked permission. He always asked if it would be too much of an inconvenience if the fish gathered there the next day and swam around for a few hours under the gray sky. And they had to know the element of danger that was involved because there would be nets and the bottom of the boat is somewhat sharp so they may bump up against it. They had to know the consequences.

Apparently it didn't matter. Madigan peered through the choppy waters and saw a flash of silver. And then another flash. Apparently they appreciated Jacob's respectful request and figured they had lived long enough already. They gathered around the edge of the boat, looking up at Madigan with their motionless eyes. They didn't need sympathy. Better a net and price for their head than some lucky cat or a wave that dashes them against a cliff. *Yes, a net was better*, they had decided.

Jacob glanced up into the shining sky. It wasn't raining yet. He looked over the boat's edge. Thread by thread he caressed the net. Each thread had a name. Every fiber had a thought behind it. The wind stopped and hovered over the boat. The fish waited beneath the waves, their faces pointed upwards. Madigan focused her eyes so that she could keep both her father's face and hands in sight. His fingers were feeling their way along the silky pathways and his peaceful face was telling so many stories she couldn't catch them all.

Fiber by fiber, each thread flushed gold with excitement. Jacob stood up in the boat and the ocean clamped its gray fingers around the boat's edges so it wouldn't rock. He shook out the nets and tossed them into the air as simply as that. The wind reached out and straightened the nets so that it landed atop the waves in a perfect oval. The nets disappeared beneath the surface just that way, the unfortunate collector off to do its duty. Jacob raised his hands and smoothed them over his head. He watched his nets disappear into the ocean depths, his face dark with what he was tasked to do. He sat down and closed his eyes, hands cupped behind his neck as he leaned back against the railing of the boat.

Father and daughter waited in silence. Jacob occasionally peered over the side of the boat but would return back to his relaxed stance, settling in with a long sigh. When she thought he wasn't looking, Madigan would take a peek into the water herself. She could see the net, floating wispily beneath the waves. One by one, the fish gathered and congregated within the confines of the net, choosing entanglement over life. Madigan returned back to her seat, unsettled by what she had seen. She formed the words in her head carefully before interrupting her father's light doze.

"Papa," she began, already regretting what she about to ask. She could anticipate the lengthy explanation about the elements before Jacob even said it. "What exactly…are you doing?"

Jacob opened one eye and looked at his daughter. "Waiting for the nets to fill up," he replied, closing his eye again.

"Why are the fish doing this?"

"I simply ask and the fish listen. It's their choice, but they are good little creatures. They understand."

Surprised by these unusually short responses, Madigan found herself asking more. "But what do you *say* to them?"

Clearing his throat as he sat up, Jacob rubbed his face awake. He looked up at her with a grin, one eyebrow arched very high. "You really want to know?" Before Madigan could respond he continued on, rubbing his hands together. "I tell them the whole story and every bit of it is true. I tell them my family needs them to survive. I tell them the story of all of us. And you may not believe it now, but they do care. One generation dies and sets the example for the next and so on and so on. I can do all this because the sea is my conduit. My interpreter. It translates my words so they can understand it. And we never take too much. Never."

Jacob settled back in his seat, watching his daughter's expression. Madigan wasn't surprised by any of it, she had some semblance of understanding already. But to hear her father express the process made it feel real. The boat jerked suddenly and Jacob pushed back his cap.

"That'll be them. Sit back," he ordered, pushing up his sleeves as he reached into the water. With a grunt, he began to pull up the net handful by handful until the top layers of fish began to poke through. Madigan didn't like this part. They wriggled in the air horribly and she wondered if they regretted their decision at all. With one last heave, Jacob pulled the net completely into the boat that now rattled with flopping fish. He stood very still until the last fish had died then he sat down, solemnly placing the oars back in the water and rowing towards home. Madigan stared at the boat full of fish, reaching down to touch the net. She felt the gritty fibers between her fingertips, still damp and glistening. She looked up at her father.

"My net?" he asked, anticipating her question. He winked. "Well, that's another story."

VIII

THE MORNING

"**A**re you ready?"

Jacob was standing by the empty sink, the morning light coming in slanted through the window. He had a milky white coffee cup cradled between his hands. But there wasn't any coffee in it. Coffee was too gravelly and grainy for the fisherfolk, it was too much like the soil. Instead, they would drink tea made on the porch beneath the afternoon sun or simply water, like Jacob. Jacob was simply water.

Madigan couldn't stop smiling. *It was May Day.* She looked down at herself, sitting on the floor. Yes, she was ready. Each year, in the dead winter months, Elise and she would plan and measure for Madigan's May Day dress. It was the best cure for those dull winter months when the gloom gathered around the windows to watch and see what was going on. And each year, Madigan would know exactly what she wanted and Elise gave it to her. One year, she wanted to look like a summer sunset and Elise gave it to her. Or the falling rain. Or the darkest shadow. With the help of her needle and thread, Elise gave them to her.

This year, Madigan wanted to be the sea. They adjusted the color of the dye in big buckets in the front yard, staining their hands with the indigo ink. But what was the sea without sand. Madigan and Elise had gone to the beach together and filled their cupped hands with the richest and oldest sand they could find, sprinkling it over the damp fabric. After that, only the final step remained. Madigan laid her dress across the wet sand and the ocean reached out and washed over it. The salt added the final bit of magic by gently dispersing the sand grains, leaving the best and brightest for Madigan's dress. The rest of the sand was washed back into the sea so it could make itself better for another day.

"Yes, I'm ready," Madigan announced, fingering the shells pinned to her hair. Today, she really was the sea.

Jacob smiled as he took another sip from the milky white coffee cup. He was always the sea. His expressions were like breakers crashing against the beach and the stubble on his cheeks resembled dark pieces of sand. His brown khaki pants were rolled up around his ankles as though he had been wading through the tide. His hair was like the water at night, the darkest blue in the absence of light.

Henry burst into the living room, chasing after his youngest sister. "Sara, get back here!" he shouted as she slipped through his grasp.

"Hi, Charlie!" Sara giggled as she plopped down on the floor. She was wearing Madigan's old rain droplets dress that was pale watery blue with snowflake stitching around the hem. Her hair was falling down from where it had only been partially braided.

Henry stood in the kitchen, panting. "Mama told me to braid her hair but she won't sit still! You do it, Maddie," he grumbled.

"But he was doing it with the wind! I don't want a wind braid. I want a *real* braid!" Sara pouted, knocking the tips of her bare toes together.

"Shush, you're getting a real braid," Madigan whispered, tugging on her sister's hair for extra incentive to keep quiet. She snuck a quick glance at her father. She could feel her brother's dread from across the room.

Jacob cleared his throat and set the milky white coffee cup on the kitchen counter, turning to face his son. They were almost the same height and it appeared to catch Jacob off guard. Henry pretended to keep eye contact but Madigan guessed he was probably looking just over the top of his father's head.

"You were using the wind to braid your sister's hair?" Jacob repeated.

"Yes," Henry replied with a shrug.

Jacob pursed his lips together and sniffed. "Do you think that was wise?"

"Why shouldn't I? Besides, I need to get my practice and this stupid festival is keeping me from it," Henry responded snappishly. His dark hair bristled like he had been using the wind to style it as well. He was dressed like Jacob, strangely enough. It was strange because he never made that attempt before. Maybe it was just May Day. Maybe May Day just had that way.

Madigan continued to braid Sara's hair, her fingers stiffening. *Not today. Please, not that day.* Of all the days they could stare at each other and fight about the use of the wind, not May Day. She breathed a sigh of relief when Elise entered the kitchen. She entered like the sun, burning off the tense fog with just a few scattered rays of light. She passed by, dropping a stiff rubber band and a few hair pins down by her daughter's side just as Madigan's fingers bumped together, signaling the end of the braid. She had come just in time.

"My family…" Elise whispered, holding out her arms. *She really was the sun,* Madigan thought. Tall and long in her floor-length dress, she was wispy in pale shades of yellow, her hair braided far down her back.

Madigan patted Sara on the shoulder to signal she was done with her hair. Sara bounded around the room since Elise had effectively broken the tension and now Jacob and Henry were making strained conversation. She turned and slowly looked Madigan up and down.

"You do look like the sea, Charlotte," she whispered, her eyes beginning to tear. She reached out and touched the shells in her daughter's hair, fingering them carefully. "I see it in you."

"Let's just go, all right?" Henry blustered, brushing past Elise and Madigan. "Then we can leave early." He stomped through the front door, leaving it swinging open. Madigan's dress gave a big kick at the introduction of wind.

"No! I don't want to leave early. Hear me, Henry? Papa, no!" Sara shouted loudly, following her brother out the door with a whisk of her rain droplet dress. She tugged on Jacob's big arm and dragged him with her, his loud laugh bellowing through the air.

Elise interlocked her arm with her daughter's, a moment of tenderness that surprised Madigan. They paused in the doorway.

"Can I meet you there?" Madigan ventured carefully. "There's something I need to do first."

"It must be very important to keep you from May Day," Elise said softly, a smile pulling at the corner of her lips. She removed her arm and walked through the door. She glowed as the sun caught her dress. "But I will see you there."

Madigan smiled and gathered her dress in her arms. She ran across the front yard, glancing down at her family as they began their trek to the beach. Henry was skulking ahead first with Sara stumbling after him, kicking at the sand when it snickered and tripped her. Jacob hummed an old tune and pretended to play the fiddle as he skipped along. Elise followed last, her thin hands folded neatly. She paused before descending over the last dune and looked over her shoulder at her house.

Madigan crunched through the early morning grass, each blade crystallized with dew. Once the sun had fully risen, the dew would unthaw and become liquid then evaporate away. To-day was May Day and nothing was going to ruin it for her. She turned down Shrunken Hollow Road, carefully avoiding the pot-holes full of muddy water. She hadn't seen Shogun for a week. If he was going to miss May Day, he could at least see her dress.

Carefully laboring up the slippery steps to the front door of the Saban house, Madigan inspected the doorstep that was cov-ered with a mat of moss and deemed it clean enough for her dress. Brilliant green ivy dripped down towards the doorbell that didn't work. She raised her hand and banged on the door loud-ly as was usually necessary for old Roland's failing hearing. She waited and knocked again, louder as she grew impatient. She reached her hand out again just as the door swung open. Paddie stood in the doorway, coffee cup in hand. The steam rose and curled around his face.

"Yes?" he asked as he took a sip of what was undoubtedly coffee, gravelly and grainy just like the woodsmen liked it. His voice became magnified in the depths of the dark cup. He stared at Madigan straight in the face, as though he didn't even notice her May Day dress. Or care.

"Is Shogun home?" Madigan panted, still breathless from her run. She tried to peer around Paddie's thick frame into the house. She could only see Roland standing in the kitchen, his back to her as he looked out the window.

"He can't see you right now," Paddie replied, beginning to shut the door.

"Wait!" Madigan cried out, her hand stopping the door. She felt the hairs on her neck stand at attention as Paddie looked down at her. His eyes were very dark, as though the pupil had taken over his iris. Madigan slowly removed her hand from the door.

"I gave you your answer," Paddie said sternly. "Go. Now."

"But today is May Day!" Madigan exclaimed. She touched the shells in her hair and their rigid hills and valleys rubbed against her fingertips. She needed strength for what she was about to ask. "Can Shogun please come with me?"

Madigan expected the usual response that she received every year when she asked that question. That they were busy or sick or it just wasn't their type of festivity. She wasn't expecting it when Paddie's hand reached out and slapped her face, so hard that she went stumbling down the slimy front steps. Her head rushed as she heard shouts within the house and Paddie was pulled inside. Roland appeared in the doorway and rushed down the steps.

"Ah, girl," he whispered, helping her stand up. "I'm sorry."

Madigan gingerly touched her red cheek. She brushed off her dress as she fought back the tears. Roland bent down and picked up the shell that had fallen from Madigan's hair, now broken into several pieces. His rough hands examined them.

"I can fix it," Roland whispered, tucking them in his pocket. He looked up at the closed door. "You best get going."

Shaking her head, Madigan wiped away her tears furiously. "Where is Shogun?" she whispered.

Roland walked back up the steps slowly, hesitating before opening the door. His back looked hunched over with a thousand thoughts. He looked over his shoulder at Madigan. "Still looking out for him, I see. You're a good one, Charlotte Madigan." He opened the door. "But you should leave."

The door shut firmly and locked. Madigan stared at it, her face still smarting from Paddie's strike. She could hear more shouts inside, the deep voices of Roland and Paddie escalating until the walls threatened to crack. She took a few steps back and looked over to Shogun's bedroom window. The curtains were drawn and the light appeared to be off. Quickly picking up her dress, Madigan crouched down beneath the living room window and crept towards Shogun's room, staying close to the house.

"Shogun!" she whispered loudly, trying to peer through the cracks in the curtain. She thought he could see Shogun's leg outstretched on the bed but nothing else. Madigan tapped on the window as loud as she dared. "Shogun! Are you alright?" She breathed a heavy sigh when Shogun's leg moved.

The voices of Roland and Paddie were growing louder and Madigan's heart leapt in her chest at the sound of it. She would much rather be at May Day than dealing with these woodsmen. She pulled another shell from her hair and tucked it into the screen outside Shogun's window. At least she knew Shogun was alive. Maybe he would wake up and remember that today was May Day and anything was possible.

Madigan cut through the trees and returned to Shrunken Hollow Road. She looked behind her one last time but the house had retreated into the shadows, as though wrapping its arms around itself. She turned and ran so fast that she was always on the verge of tripping, but she didn't. She ran towards the sea through clouds of steamy mist as the morning dew was burned off by the emerging sun. The moisture gathered on her face, washing away the sting of Paddie's hand. She breathed in. She breathed out. Today was May Day and nothing would ruin it for her.

IX

THE AFTERNOON

He dreamed he had heard a voice, very far in the distance. It said his name twice, each syllable drawn out and ending with a whisper. Shogun lifted his heavy head from his sweaty pillow. His room was dark with cracks of light spilling through the drawn curtains. He groaned as he rolled stiffly to the edge of the bed. He had been sleeping again. There wasn't much else to do while stuck in his room, banished due to his disobedience. He would be there until Paddie decided it had been long enough. This had happened times before, but long enough had never been this long. Shogun stood up and opened his door slightly. Paddie didn't have to lock it, he knew his son wouldn't dare leave.

The house was quiet. Shogun could hear the ticking of the old wood clock around the corner. He could tell by the way the light stretched across the floor that it was the afternoon. Roland sat at the kitchen table, only his hunched back visible. He stretched and Shogun could see he was holding a small can of glue and a brush. The sliding glass door opened and Shogun quickly shut his door. He pressed his ear to the wood and listened.

"I need some help out there," Paddie ordered. His heavy foot-steps paced in the kitchen. There was a slap as he shook off his gloves and then the hum of the refrigerator.

There was no response from Roland other than the creaks of the chair as he repositioned.

"Hear me?" Paddie said louder.

"Aye," Roland responded calmly. "But I'm not helping you."

Shogun raised an eyebrow and pressed his ear against the door harder.

"What are you saying?" Paddie's tone was tense.

"Do it yourself. All of you."

"Lazy traitor."

"I want no part of this!" Roland shouted suddenly, followed by a rush of papers fluttering through the air. One of the kitchen table chairs scratched violently across the floor and there was a struggle. Shogun put his hand on the doorknob but stopped when he heard them both take a breath and release.

"You…" Roland puffed. "There is something wrong with you, son."

"What's wrong with me," Paddie replied shrilly. "Is that I've taken this long to see it. Those damn fisherfolk with their elementals. It's what charmed Tara, you know it! She was obsessed!"

"Tara had an accident!" Roland bellowed. "She fell! Yes, from the trees. Yes, her fisherfolk friend encouraged her. Yes, she loved it. But it was an accident, that is all! Get over it!"

Shogun went cold. It was not often he heard his mother's name mentioned in that house. He dropped to the ground so he could hear better.

"It's all happening again," Paddie whispered. There were footsteps across the floor and papers scattering beneath them. "Shogun. The trees. That evil girl. If I don't stop it now, I'll lose him too."

"No. No, Paddie," Roland sighed heavily. Shogun heard the creak of the chair as his grandfather sat down. "I just don't understand," he muttered.

There were several beats of silence. Something was picked up from the table, Shogun could hear as it was dragged across the wood.

"What is this?" Paddie asked slowly. *"A shell?"*

"You struck a little girl," Roland seethed. "Yes, I'm going to fix that damn dammit shell for her if it's the last thing I do!"

"Be careful when you say things like that," Paddie whispered. He threw the shell on the ground and there was a sickening crack as he smashed it into the floor with his boot. "Or they may come true."

The sliding glass door opened and Shogun heard his father's thundering footsteps leave the house. Then there was the unmistakable spark as Roland lit his pipe. He groaned as he stood up and Shogun could hear as he approached his grandson's room. Backing up against his bed, Shogun watched the outline of grandfather's boots as he stood outside the door. There was a click of a lock and then Roland hesitated. Shogun heard the rough sandpaper of his hand as it slid down the wood door frame. The footsteps retreated and the sliding glass door opened one last time. Then there was silence again. Shogun tried his doorknob. Locked.

Running to his bed, Shogun jumped up and swept aside the thick curtains. He peered through the window as Roland and Paddie climbed into their old truck and drove off in the direction of Paddie's work shed. As he unlocked and opened his window, Shogun found something caught in the tracks. A shell, brushed and polished clean of all evidence of the sea. A small bobby pin was glued to the back side. There was only one person who would wear this and now Shogun remembered why. It must be May Day. He examined the shell in his hand and thought to the one lying as dust on his kitchen floor. His heart began to race.

Breaking through the screen, Shogun crawled through the window and dropped to the ground. He stayed low, listening for the truck. Hearing nothing, Shogun ran around the house to the sliding glass door. That door was never locked because it couldn't. It wouldn't, they had never even tried. He quickly snuck into the house and shut the door behind him. His bare feet crunched across a dozen pieces of paper, strewn across the kitchen floor just as he had imagined it. He picked up one piece and found a map of familiar road names and points. He picked up another and found a page of dark drawings, scribbles of screams and pain. He found plans and diagrams for a cage with polaroids attached that documented the cage's progress. Shogun's heart began to beat furiously against his ribs. They were taken at his father's work shed. Then a draft of a letter. Each sentence gained in hysteria as the letter went on. A letter to Paddie's comrades, urging them to help him rid them of the fisherfolk, once and for all.

In a flurry, Shogun gathered the papers in his arms and burst out of the house. He had never run like that before. He felt like he was chasing the light as it quickly began its descent into night. *Not yet.* He had to get to them. He had to get to May Day.

He was not far from his house when Shogun tripped and landed in an explosion of papers. He exclaimed and slammed his fists into the ground. When he tried to stand again, he found that both wrists had been wrapped by a tree root. As he tried to pull himself free, he felt the scaly skin of ivy crawl up his back. It began to pull him down gently, piling atop his shoulders until his back was on the ground. His head rested in a cocoon of soft moss, filling his senses with the smell of damp soil that was suffocating and relaxing at the same time.

"Wait..." Shogun whispered as he slipped into a sliver of consciousness.

As his heart rate began to drop into hibernation, a sprinkling of young leaves fell from the trees, covering him in a blanket of spring. It continued this way until only the tip of Shogun's face remained above the ground, hidden and tucked safely in their arms, just as the forest wanted him. He can't fight this. *Not yet.*

X

THE NIGHT

Madigan looked over her shoulder. *Say it again.* Once more, slowly. She narrowed her eyes in strained thought as she listened. The night ocean had said something small that made her turn and look from beside the bonfire. She took a slow, long sip of her hot apple cider as if its striking taste would help her hear more clearly. The message was not repeated again although she had asked and she had listened. Madigan looked up to the sky but saw nothing alarming. She took another swig of the cider and relaxed. *It was just the night,* the bonfire told her.

It had been a good May Day. She had left the episode at the Saban house behind, her face no longer red once her feet stepped upon the sand. Her family and friends had danced all day, to the point she thought her legs would give out. Once sunset arrived they ate and drank so much that they slept across the warm sand, gearing up for the second round of celebrating that commenced once the sun went to sleep. Even the moon stayed out of it, not fond of having to compete for attention.

The evening sky was finally replaced by the night. The trees could now only offer their dark silhouettes, gathered around the edges of the light like sleeping statues. The wind was lurking through their shadows, free to roam on this night that belonged to the elements. The beach was scattered with fisherfolk dressed in their festive costumes, laughing and singing across the sand. This was their night to celebrate. To honor the good that outweighed the bad. A large bonfire had been built and surrounded by pieces of driftwood so the older fisherfolk could rest and be warm. Its ashes were ancient. When May Day was over and the fisherfolk buried the coals, the old embers remained there year after year, burning beneath the sand.

There, again. Madigan tightened her grip around her mug, not daring to turn and look. It took a certain kind of ear and a certain state of mind to understand what she was hearing. She pushed harder and harder, sweat gathering on her forehead. Her body began to tremble with the exertion. She held her breath as her eyes focused on the bonfire. *She felt it.* The loud concoction of voices around her faded into a distant murmur and the cider mug slipped out of her hands.

Madigan stumbled through the faces in the crowd, their laughter and singing blurring together as she searched for her father. Tears began to gather on the edges of her eyelids and they fell down her face like rain. Finally, she found Jacob standing in a circle with his friends, his arms high in the air as he told a story. Madigan broke through breathlessly, falling at his feet.

"Maddie, what is it?" Jacob demanded, crouching down next to her. His face had gone ashen even in the red of the firelight.

Madigan couldn't talk. She tried to but the terror in her chest kept closing in and stopping her. *Please let her be wrong.* Jacob stared at her solemnly. He turned his head slightly, an ear towards the sea. Madigan watched his expression change until he met her gaze again. She began to sob uncontrollably. She had heard it right.

Elise appeared and grabbed Jacob by the shoulder, turning him around. Her eyes were huge and the grip on Sara's hand by her side was so tight it looked painful.

"We have to run!" she whispered loudly. A slow and steady panic had begun to spread through the crowd, igniting like a wildfire. The others were hearing it, too. "Now!"

"I have to find Henry," he said firmly. He reached out and touched his wife's face. "I'll meet you at the house."

Madigan jumped up and wrapped her arms around her father's chest. He smelled like the apple cider.

"No! No!" she wailed so loudly that the panicked voices around them became background noise. Jacob pulled back Madigan's head so he could look at her.

"You heard it first. I knew you were the strongest," he whispered tearfully, attempting a smile. "Go with your mother."

"Come, Charlotte," Elise ordered, grabbing her daughter's hand. Madigan pulled it away.

"What do you mean? We can't leave them!" she cried out.

Screams broke out due to a commotion behind the dunes. Madigan turned and saw a fireworks display of flashing lights and thick clouds of sand splashing through the air. Along the horizon of the dunes, silhouette after silhouette lined up shoulder to shoulder. Lit by the light of the bright lanterns, a giant cage was dragged over the dunes by horses that tripped and tumbled in the loose sand. There was a pause, so electric that the air seemed to crackle, and then a great shout as the silhouettes became screaming men running down the dunes. The crowds scattered in a frenzy, screaming and pushing away anyone in their path.

Suddenly, Madigan's family was gone. She held her head between her hands. There were so many voices all calling out at the same time that the air became muddled with confusion that even the wind could not separate. There were terrified faces everywhere. Some dove into the angry sea while others ran hopelessly towards the bonfire. Madigan caught the quickest glimpse of Jacob and ran after his sweaty cotton shirt.

She halted as she spotted her brother. Henry and a woodsmen were struggling against each other. A group of stunned fisherfolk had gathered around, hoping that the safety in numbers would protect them from the screams on the far away edges. Henry broke free and called a great gust of wind that knocked down his opponent. The woodsmen jumped up again and ran swinging and shouting at Henry, his blade cutting through the air.

"Stop!" Jacob shouted from the crowd. He stepped between Henry and the woodsman. As he held up his hands, the woodsman cautiously lowered his sword. "Stop! Please!"

"We won't stop!" a man's voice shouted from within the group of woodsmen. He pushed his way up to the front and faced Jacob. Madigan felt her throat tighten as she recognized Paddie Saban. The crowd hushed and froze, pausing to listen to the exchange between the two men.

"*Paddie?*" Jacob gasped, his eyes wide. He shook his head and held up his hands helplessly. "What can you possibly be thinking?"

"I've had enough, Jake," Paddie said coolly. He crossed his arms over his chest then slowly lowered one of his hands to the hilt of his sheathed sword.

"He has a sword!" Madigan screamed, taking a few steps forward. Paddie's head snapped in her direction and she saw the reflection of the bonfire erupting in his black eyes.

"That's the problem. Right there!" he shouted, pointing at Madigan. He looked around himself and pointed at another fisherfolk, then another, then another. "All of you! You're infecting us with your filthy religion and we won't lose another of our own to it!"

Jacob's chest was heaving with deep breaths. "We are brothers, Paddie. In our own way, we are brothers," he insisted loudly and passionately. The wind whipped his face wildly, carrying to him the thoughts of all the fisherfolk gathered on the beach. "Don't follow this path any further. It will consume you."

"I will consume you first," Paddie seethed. There was a melody of high-pitched metal as the swords of the woodsmen were drawn. Paddie stepped up and grabbed Jacob by the collar. "You want the sea? Now you'll die by it!"

Madigan felt herself shriek louder than her voice could afford and the end fell into a broken whisper. There was a loud rumbling as the cage was rolled into the center of the crowd. Another troop of woodsmen emerged from the outskirts of the crowd, advancing towards any fisherfolk they could catch. A hand grabbed Madigan and for a moment she believed this was the end of her existence.

"Run, now! Hide!" It was Roland Saban. Madigan would have recognized the heavy scent of pipe smoke anywhere. Unable to control herself, she threw herself at him and held tight.

"What's happening?" she cried.

Roland held her back and looked right into her eyes. "No matter what, don't watch," he whispered. "Now, go!"

Madigan ran. She ran to the outskirts of the beach, where the sand and the rocks mixed and cut her bare feet. She dropped and hid beneath a sleeping tree, protected by its limp branches. Crawling on her belly, Madigan watched as dozens of fisherfolk were shoved into the cage, some toppling over each other while others dove for the bars and attacked them in vain. The crowd became a blur until Madigan spotted her father and brother, led into the cage by Paddie himself. The door slammed behind them.

"There! That's all we can fit!" Paddie shouted to the other woodsmen. He looked around at the remaining fisherfolk who stumbled away. "Another day for them!" he dismissed. "Alright, go!"

With a crack of a whip, the nervous horses began toiling through the sand towards the sea. Madigan covered her mouth to quiet her sobs. She closed her eyes the instant she heard splashing. *No matter what, don't watch*. Her eyes filled with tears and they slipped down her face like the rivers that feed the sea. Down her face, moistening the soft skin of her neck and saturating the collar of her sea dress.

Now she hated her dress. Now that the sea was slowly eating its way through the submerged bodies, Madigan wished there was no sea. She wanted to escape forever to the place behind her closed eyes, a place where there was no sea or sky or sand or wind or cage. A place she could hide in. She would go there now, to the darkness. Those were not screams she was hearing. That was not the sound of hands reaching above the waves, grasping for air. In that dark place, she could breathe. In and out. In and out. In that dark place, the elements could not speak.

XI

THE FATHER AND THE SON

He inhaled deeply. The first sense to awaken was Shogun's sense of smell. The damp moss that covered his face had gathered beneath his nostrils, waving back and forth with each inhale and exhale. Then he could taste the dew layered between his teeth, gritty with minuscule pieces of soil. Shogun blinked rapidly as his eyes adjusted to the early morning light slanting through the trees. Finally, he began to hear the sounds of the forest, slowly stretching awake after a long night's sleep. His mind felt thick and his muscles stiff and weak. Turning his head, he looked over at the plans for May Day scattered across the forest floor. The ink had almost completely dissolved, washed away by the moisture of the night. He closed his eyes and remembered.

Shogun sat up when he heard the sound of an approaching truck. He ripped the remaining roots and leaves from his body and crawled to the edge of the forest. He wiped the dirt from his eyelashes as the family truck pulled in front of the house and the engine ticked to a stop. Paddie exited the vehicle briskly, reaching into the trunk to remove several armfuls of rope. Roland followed, his back hunched over as he leaned against the truck for support, as though the weight of his body was too much for him to handle. Paddie brushed by him, throwing the ropes to the side of the house.

"Go to bed, old man," Paddie grumbled, continuing to unpack tools from the trunk. He threw them to the ground with a loud clatter.

"Go to bed," Roland repeated sourly, looking down at his hands. "As if I could sleep after what we've just done."

"I will sleep just fine," Paddie sighed, wiping his hands through his hair.

"Aye, I know you will," Roland said loudly, grabbing his son by the shoulder. He looked in his face wildly. "And that is what's wrong with you."

"Hands off," Paddie bristled, pushing Roland to the ground. "I've had just about enough of you."

Roland rose stiffly from the ground. Shogun could feel the pain in his grandfather's knees as he held onto the truck to help him stand. His other hand held his sword firmly, the rising blade catching the morning light. He lifted it and pointed it at Paddie, the tip wavering. "And I've had enough of you, whatever you are. But you are not my son."

Paddie reached for his own sword, locked in its sheath. His hand remained there, resting on the hilt.

"Go to bed," Paddie repeated firmly.

"Aye, I will. But I have one thing to do first."

Shogun instinctively ducked as Roland raised his sword and swung at Paddie, who jumped easily out of the way. He slapped away Roland's blade with his own, the clank of the metal meeting metal ringing through the quiet morning air. They continued this way for a breathless minute, straining against each other and tripping through the loose soil of the driveway. Shogun's heart beat faster with every strike. He could tell Roland was growing very weary while Paddie only seemed to grow stronger with each blow. Shogun had never seen his father with a sword before. It amazed him and terrified him at the same time.

Suddenly, time seemed to stand still. The trees towered above them in silence, watching. Waiting. Paddie took a long breath and drew the sword back. He shouted as he pierced the blade into Roland's ribcage. When he drew it out, Roland dropped to the ground, groaning and cursing as he fell. He pressed the sight of the wound and Shogun could see the bright red blood dripping from his hand. Paddie buckled over, panting as he tried to catch his breath.

"Didn't know you had it in you…" Roland laughed, blood sputtering from his mouth. He coughed and rolled onto this back.

Paddie walked over and kicked a cloud of dirt into Roland's face. He knelt down and whispered something to his father, words strong enough to make the old man shout and try to stand up. Paddie turned and walked back towards the house, shutting the door behind him.

Shogun was up and running the moment the door closed. The trees tried to reach out for him but he was too fast, sliding to a stop next to his grandfather. Roland's face looked gray and very old as if he had been dead for a hundred years, all color dripping from his body through the wound in his side. Shogun fought back the tears and inspected the old man's face carefully. He wasn't supposed to cry, that's what Roland would have said. He felt a cold rage build inside of him. He heard his father's footsteps inside the house and each step made him bolder and bolder. Beside Roland's limp hand laid his sword. Shogun grabbed it with both hands and stood up, the blade scratching across the drive.

"Shogun…" Roland whispered hoarsely.

"Grandpa!" Shogun gasped, tears streaming down his face as he knelt beside the old man. He shook his head, crying angrily as he dropped the sword to hold Roland's hand.

Roland's labored breathing grew louder. "Don't...go in there," he warned.

"I want to kill him," Shogun whispered fiercely. "Why is he...?"

"You can't," Roland moaned quietly. "Let me know...that you live." He squeezed Shogun's hand with the last of his strength, pulling him down closer. *"Get strong...then come back."*

Shogun looked up as he heard his bedroom door open. He would have recognized the squeak of the door anywhere. The forest sparked to life at once and the house cried out an alert as Paddie raged. *Shogun was gone.*

"Go...go..." Roland urged, pushing his grandson away. "The trees will guide you. Go!"

Roland collapsed and Shogun ran for the woods, looking back one last time to see that his grandfather was truly gone, left to join the other wandering spirits. He kept running, following the secret paths that only he knew. The forest ran along with him, covering his tracks and asking the wind to propel him forward faster and faster. He didn't know if his father was following him. He didn't stop to look. Every fiber in his body said to run. He heard the chants of his grandfather in his mind, urging him on further and further.

Ahead, Shogun saw a break in the trees. As he drew closer, he identified it as an old logging road, overgrown with bushes. The grooves in the road from the heavy vehicles were filled with moss and weeds. Cautiously stepping onto the loose gravel, Shogun stopped to catch his breath. He looked up as he heard a strange sound in the still air. To his side stood a post with a gathering of small flower buds beneath it. The top of the sign was covered with thick fir needles. The wind rustled the branches, scratching and brushing the needles across a wooden sign. Shogun moved the branches out of the way. This was a bus stop.

Shogun's ear twitched at the sound of a faraway motor. He quickly pulled his hood over his head and ducked back into the woods. It sounded like a large vehicle, its engine sputtering and hissing as it chugged along the rough logging road. Soon a cloud of introductory dust wafted into Shogun's field of view. It was followed by a front bumper and a well-tread tire. The brakes let out a discontented screech.

His hood flew back as the door of the bus swung open and released a burst of air. Shogun blinked a few times and stared at the strange vehicle. It was tall and angular with windows scuffed from cloudy mysterious silhouettes. There was a neat looking, older woman sitting in the stiff black leather driver's seat. In front of her was a giant black steering wheel, grasped so hard that it was left with perfect indentations in perfect positions. The woman was extraordinarily neat in the way her grayish hair was pulled back in a perfect bun and how the contrasting colors of her green shirt and blue pants subtly matched. Her nose was angular like the bus as though she had intended that to subtly match, as well. She turned off the engine and glowed down at Shogun, clicking her pink tongue as she smiled.

"Hi there, baby. Where you headed?" she drawled loudly, as though she still needed to shout over the sound of the engine.

Shogun swallowed hard and shrugged. He looked around at the forest and exchanged glances. "I don't know," he answered.

The bus driver titled her head to the side quizzically. The left corner of her enormous Cheshire cat grin began to twitch and her tongue clicked as she repeated Shogun. "*I don't know*, eh? Well, baby, my name's Meadowsweet and I've never heard of a place like that!"

Shogun said nothing. He climbed out from his hiding place within the trees and brushed himself off. He felt small beneath Meadowsweet's perch at the top of the bus. She looked Shogun up and down carefully, glancing up at the roof of the bus without moving her head. Slowly and with much effort, she lowered her lips over her teeth and what remained was a much smaller, relaxed smile. Several different expressions flashed across her face, as though she was conversing with the roof of the bus.

"You're Shogun, right?" Meadowsweet said sweetly. There were little wrinkles all around the corners of her mouth where the skin had been stretched by larger grins.

Shogun blinked. "How did you know my name?"

"Let's just say you looked like a Shogun. Now, hop in!" Her smile clicked and the engine roared. She winked and a little bell rang somewhere in the distance.

Shogun hesitated and looked over his shoulder. The forest had sufficiently erased all trace of him, to the point he couldn't even remember how he got there. They had even wiped it from their own memories, a time and a place they wanted to forget. There was no going back even if he tried. Even if he wanted to.

Meadowsweet watched him, leaning forward in her seat with anticipation. She sighed as Shogun reached out and grabbed the side of the bus, climbing the chipping yellow steps one a time. "Right on, baby. Right on," she cheered.

As he passed through the cab of the bus, making uncertain eye contact, Shogun realized the smiling bus driver really did smell meadow sweet. The vehicle was completely empty except for the vacant seats and an aisle covered with a non-slip surface that stretched along the length of the bus. Little clouds of dust floated happily through the air, breaking their chatter only to acknowledge Shogun with a look in his direction.

Meadowsweet turned around in her seat to watch Shogun stumble through the bus cautiously. Her clicking smile and her bell-ringing wink fired simultaneously as she hollered across the bus. "Don't mind the dust sprites! They're a little shy of strangers. Had their hearts broken too many times, I suspect."

Shogun stopped mid-decision on what seat to choose and turned to look at Meadowsweet. "What?"

Meadowsweet sat up straighter in the driver's seat. "Well, this isn't just a bus, you know. To the dust sprites, this is their home."

As she spoke, Shogun felt a shy tickle around his ears as the dust sprites began to examine him closely. He froze, afraid to move.

Meadowsweet continued talking as though this was just part of the protocol. "What would you think if someone made themselves comfortable in your home, then just up and left without an explanation? They don't understand final destinations, baby. So just be patient with them."

Shogun attempted to do that but began to wonder if the dust sprites were prodding a bit too far into his ears. The flesh beneath his fingernails began to tingle and his hair began to fluff as each strand stood on end. Then, like a great gust of wind, the dust sprites returned to the air and Shogun was left with the last lingering of the sensations. He collapsed on the nearest seat and licked his lips. He could taste dust, lime, and chewing gum.

"Yeah, they leave a bit of a taste in your mouth, don't they? Oh well. They don't mean it, and besides, that means they like you," Meadowsweet laughed, turning back towards the front dash of the bus.

The bus glided to a start then began to accelerate as it raced down the logging road in a cloud of dirt. Meadowsweet turned on the windshield wipers to combat the flying rocks. Shogun squeezed over to the window seat and carefully wiped away the gathered dust there so he could peer through the glass.

"I don't have a radio, so you'll have to be left to your own thoughts," Meadowsweet called above the sound of the engine, which was strangely rhythmic and out of tune at the same time.

"Where are we going?" Shogun shouted back. He could see the reflection of her eyes in the rearview mirror, bobbing up and down with the bouncing of the bus.

There was a very loud click and Shogun guessed where that came from. "Well, sweetums, I'm heading north for my next stop! We'll find somewhere to drop you off. Don't you worry!"

Now the bus was driving so fast that the trees blurred into one another. Shogun closed his eyes and the dust sprites reached over to hold his hand. He pressed his face against the cold glass and felt the shadows of the forest flickering across his face, masking the tears. *Get strong…then come back.* Shogun opened his eyes and watched the trees burn into the afternoon light.

XII

THE MOTHER AND THE DAUGHTER

One key after another. Sometimes she played monotonous, three note melodies and sometimes the string of chords would create some version of a song. The dynamics changed, too. Sometimes loud and sometimes so soft that Madigan would sit and wonder if she was hearing it at all. And even though Madigan knew her mother took breaks, Elise was always there. At the piano, her legs tucked neatly under the bench, her next finger poised to execute its action as soon as the others were done. Madigan would enter the empty living room and even when the piano was closed and empty, Elise was still there, somehow.

The house was closed up and dark and hot. It was restless, forever different without Jacob and Henry. It stayed up at night and waited for them, wondering if they would come in through the door and all would be right. The night of May Day, Madigan had stumbled home in blind tears to find her mother and sister, wrapped asleep in bed. As though content with what had happened. As though accepting the blood that swirled beneath the sea. She couldn't understand it. She never would.

The dawn rose the next morning but the woodsmen never came for them. Not the next day or the next, as though the actions of May Day had been wiped from their minds completely. When they ventured out, Madigan and her sister were met with awkward glances but the world continued on the same. Elise told her to be thankful. If her family was going to survive she had to sell fish to the woodsmen. Madigan would sell them the fish. But she hoped they choked and died on them.

She slammed her breakfast bowl into the kitchen sink. Madigan meant for it to make a loud noise, hoping the distraction would cause some break in the clamor of notes. Elise's back jerked slightly at the sound but continued playing without a glitch. Madigan ground her teeth together hard, running a quick blast of water over her dirty eating utensils. She watched the murky water disappear down the drain.

At the table, Sara was seated in her small wooden chair, humming along with her mother's tune. She dropped her spoon into her empty bowl and looked expectantly at her sister. "All done! Look, Charlie! I finished it all!"

Madigan reached over and took Sara's bowl. She dropped it in the sink and looked out the kitchen window. A summer storm was coming. She watched it hovering out across the sea, waiting. *Waiting for what*, she wondered. Just come and rain and go away.

"Sara, it's time for your nap," Madigan said absently, still staring out the window. She brushed a lock of her sweaty, frizzy hair behind her ear and pulled at her sticky cotton dress. It felt plastered to her body and was damp beneath her armpits and on her abdomen.

Sara sighed heavily and scooted her chair away from the table. "You're no fun, anymore," she mumbled as she passed by. She broke into a run upstairs, stomping across the thin floors. Madigan heard the springs on Sara's mattress squeak and guessed she was hiding under the blankets, listening for her older sister's potential approach.

The piano fell silent. "You'll be going out today, won't you, Charlotte," her mother's faint voice ventured from the living room. It wasn't a question.

Madigan looked around the corner at her mother. She glanced out the window to where the storm was still immobile. "I don't want to. There's a storm."

The piano bench creaked as Elise repositioned her weight. Her form was deep darkness now, like the rich mahogany of the piano.

"You already grow weary," she murmured. "You simply must catch the fish or you will fail. You and Sara cannot fail. Go and try again."

It had fallen on Madigan to pick up the nets and go back to the sea, a role meant for Henry now dropped on her. Madigan leaned her head back and combed her fingers through her tangled hair. Her sweaty, sticky hair. She felt like the whole world was closing in on her, making her suffocate with its noxious breath. She inhaled and shook her head, fighting back the tears.

Her mother began to turn around in her seat. Elise's face was gaunter than it had been the night before, the circles under her eyes the hue of a midnight blue sky. The stars in her eyes were dimming to nothing. Madigan stared at her and walked closer.

Elise sighed and looked down at her calloused hands. "Finally, you see."

"What's happening to you?" Madigan whispered, kneeling down in front of her mother. She looked at her bony knees protruding through the fabric of her dress, as though she was melting away.

"Go out again," Elise whispered. She grabbed Madigan's hand and squeezed it hard. "No matter what, survive. You *must*."

Madigan stood up. A panic rose in her stomach, burning up her throat. She could not avoid it any longer. She had gone to Jacob's fishing boat many times but could not bring herself to disturb it. She would climb in and touch the sleeping nets, neatly piled under the seats of the boat. She ran her hands over the oars and the edging of the craft, sliding her fingertips over the imprint of his. But it could not wait any longer. She walked to the door and stepped into her boots, pulling her hoodie over her dress. Madigan placed her hand on the seashell doorknob and hesitated, looking over her shoulder at her mother.

"I'll be here when you get back," Elise assured.

Madigan ran to the beach, breathlessly stopping a few inches from Jacob's boat. The hovering storm on the horizon was now approaching fast. The wind pushed her hair out of her eyes. Madigan felt relief in its salty embrace, allowing it to wipe her sweat away. She let it enter her mind, where it wailed through like a wild ghost, charging her to be strong. She braced her shoulder against the bow and pushed the small craft towards the steady waves.

Climbing into the boat, Madigan began to row hard towards the storm, her hands strong with that wood of the past. She locked the nets down below her boots and felt them tingling with life. The waves rocked the tiny craft as it contemplated and observed her. This little girl of the sea, adventuring across its deep depths. So small yet so powerful.

Once Madigan reached the storm she felt her heart flutter at the growing distance between her and the shore. The wind whipped her attention in all different directions. Making sure the nets were still secure beneath her, Madigan took one last breath and plunged into the dark clouds. When she opened her eyes she found herself in the calm of the storm, the sound of her racing breath magnified in the thick layers of fog. She reached down and pulled the nets up to her chest, as though to cover herself. *Think, Maddie. Think.*

Then she remembered. *Tell them the story.* Madigan closed her eyes and told the fish and the sea the story of the last few weeks. She told them about her hot house and her fading mother. About the cage she feared was right beneath her, opening its mouth to swallow her, too. How she couldn't sleep at night, watching through her window for the danger that never came. When she did sleep, she dreamed she starved until folding into a pile of bones. These were all things the sea already knew but it listened anyway. The fish had to hear it in her own words for it to mean anything.

She clenched the nets in her hands hard as the tears streamed off her face. They became soaked with salt water before even touching the sea. Gripping the side of the boat, Madigan leaned over and slid the nets unceremoniously beneath the water. They sank further and further into the shadows until darkness engulfed them completely. She held her breath until finally she saw a flash of light. She met the gaze of a fish, obligingly diving down into the depths of the net. Then another appeared and another, glinting as they waved good-bye and dove away.

The craft began to rock from the movement in the net. Bracing her feet against the side of the boat, Madigan plunged her hands beneath the water and began to pull on the nets, straining to bring them above the surface. Finally, they broke above the still water, filled to the limits with squirming fish. Madigan pulled on the nets hard, drawing on all her strength to pull them over the edge. They toppled to the bottom of the boat as the fish thumped hard on the wood, wildly impatient for death. She stared at them, her hands throbbing where the net had pressed into her flesh. She didn't breathe until the last fish had passed away and finally the air was still again. She reached for an oar and poked at them. They were real. She had done it.

The storm began to dissipate, as though there was no longer anything to see. Madigan labored back to shore, the craft now significantly heavier with the additional weight of the fish. When she reached the beach, she collapsed on the wet sand, her lungs burning with exertion. Once she was sure the boat was secure, Madigan left the fish in the boat and ran up to the house. When she opened the front door, a burst of air blew past her as though the hot tension was finally released. Elise was slumped against the side of the old gray couch, neatly sitting out of the way. Sara watched from the other corner, turning her head as her older sister stepped beside her.

"Mama said she went to go talk to the fishes," Sara declared, fidgeting with the fabric of the gray couch.

Madigan stared at her mother, her face frozen as her mind raced. She had to remind herself to breathe. To blink. To swallow. She turned and looked out the open door.

"You did catch the fish, didn't you?" Sara asked, leaning forward.

"Yes, I got them," Madigan whispered. She kneeled down in front of her sister, holding her small face between her hands. She searched it carefully, finding no fear or sadness.

Sara sat back against the couch and kicked her feet back and forth. "Can I go outside now? Mama said the storm's gone."

Madigan nodded. The wind blew her dress around her knees as the door shut and Sara went squealing into the fresh air. The house fell still as Madigan pulled the cover over the piano keys one last time. Her boots squished across the floor as she walked to the kitchen sink and stood there, watching her sister through the window. She gripped her shaking hands together and closed her eyes. She couldn't understand it. She never would.

PART TWO

XIII

THE WARRIORS OF RAGOON

It took his breath away. Literally, every day. There was not a sunrise it stopped for or a cloud that could stand in its way. If he stood very still, the silence would close in around him and paralyze everything but his eyes. And he would just watch and listen. After all those years, he still had not seen it all. There was always some detail he had missed. Shogun stood on the hilltop, watching the sunrise stretch across the valley. This place where the rain fell hard and the sun was always too brief. Where the trees were his ever-present companion. This place was called Ragoon.

Many falls had passed since Shogun was brought there. And he believed he was brought there. The bus driver may have dropped him off by the gates, but the trees brought him here. They had rescued him from the depths of the sea and brought him to a place that did not even exist in his dreams. Somewhere inside, he had always thought there was more to the trees but here, they knew it. They were keepers of the forest. They lived it. They breathed it. And they grew stronger because of it.

Maybe it was because Shogun had seen that valley every morning for years that it triggered so many memories. Brief, sporadic moments. He remembered waking up after that first night in Ragoon, just before the sun had risen. He was small and afraid, but then he rose the next morning and the next and the next.

Then one day he stood in that valley and he was a man. Somewhere inside had stopped clinging to the past and now he was just there, having his breath taken away.

The forest, to him, was all he needed. Shogun knew the value to each and every season, but fall always meant something more. There was something deeper about the way the trees would flush out all the colors they had held in during the summer months. Holding in. Holding back. And now that the air had signaled a change, the leaves were in true bloom. Their names and characteristics were written plainly for display, crumpling like decaying paper then falling away.

Maybe it was because Shogun had arrived in the fall that it meant so much. When everything had been an unfamiliar blur and those colors were the only clear things in his world. He remembered nights of just the wind. Beating against the side of the cabin or pushing its way beneath the door to come and touch his face. He had sunk into its bitter touch, there in his bed. Sunk lower and lower into the darkness until it was just him and the wind.

At times, he felt as though if the sky took him now, he'd be happy. He would have lived enough for any man. His past grew further and further away with each passing day. This was a place his father and grandfather had never been. A valley they could never claim. He had surpassed them in his skills, from what Shogun could remember. His muscles felt thick and hard around his arms. He could have buried the memories completely if it were not for his face. In the evening mirror, he sees their faces reflecting back at him. And in that breath before sleep, he still remembers the words. *Get strong…then come back.*

Shogun stretched and reached back for the handle of his axe that was strapped to his back. He glanced over his shoulder at the sound of footsteps, unconcerned since the trees had advised it was friend and not foe. It was Booker, his comrade from his first months in Ragoon and on. They had quickly joined forces to survive the beginning years. Booker was a match for the forest in his brown pants and a very old green sweater that was covered with fuzz. His dark shoulder length hair was always very kempt, pulled back with a piece of string.

"Morning," he said gruffly, his voice thick with sleep. He joined his friend's side, sipping a steaming cup of coffee. "I was wondering if you'd think I was one of those poachers you caught last week." His voice had a hint of teasing to it. He took another sip of coffee and shook his head, remembering his friend returning to Ragoon with the culprits tied to his horse.

Shogun smirked. He rubbed his face, remembering as well. "They would have been caught eventually."

"Eventually? Don't be modest," Booker scoffed. He paused and grew serious, stuffing his stiff fingers into his pockets. "There will be more."

Shogun nodded. He had noticed it, too. The lands around Ragoon were abandoned other than their development and the animals that lived there. But things were changing. *Hearts were changing,* the trees warned. And Shogun had seen something in those poacher's eyes that made him question where these days were going.

They turned as the remaining eldest members of Ragoon arrived in a large group, just before the morning bell summoned them. They were gathered in a cluster, blending into each other with their somewhat identical outfits and very identical hairstyles. They looked around themselves cockily as though being together in that group made them a huge, strong hand, capable of smashing anyone who came in their way.

"Shogun Saban!" a voice shouted. The crowd of men began to snicker.

Shogun looked away. He didn't care for this. It was Neal, the leader of the swarm only because he was tallest and loudest and strongest. He glowered at Booker as he approached. The moisture in the air was beginning to make the tips of his crisp brown hair glisten. He crossed his long arms over the leather vest across his chest. He squeezed in between Shogun and Booker, adjusting his sword sheath. Shogun could hear the sword rubbing against the leather and he imagined exactly where his axe was on his back. "I'm addressing you. It's rude not to respond."

Shogun did not answer. *Show them no emotion,* the trees were saying. *Show them nothing at all.*

"A bit slow this morning, aren't you?" Neal continued with a heavy sigh, backing up until he reached his comrades. He placed his hands on his hips and cocked his head to one side. "But you have been quite busy. All those mean, scary poachers you caught. Their ropes and traps must've nearly torn you to pieces!" Neal covered his mouth, feigning fear. The group roared with laughter.

Shogun let the valley feelings leave. They'd no longer belong inside of him when the anger would begin to rise. He couldn't help it, he felt it stirring and awakening inside of him. There was no reason to let the valley be tainted. He turned around to face Neal and the rest of the group. He stared at them, his face blank. Neal stopped his charade and stood up straight. He took a few more steps toward Shogun, causing Booker to stir. Shogun stayed still. *Show them no emotion. Show them nothing at all.*

"Would you just back off?" Booker bristled. "It's too early in the morning for this crap."

"I just want you to be clear," Neal murmured to Shogun, ignoring Booker. He was close enough that Shogun could smell his breath. "I see you. Think you can get a little attention by catching some trash? Try protecting Ragoon from the real predators."

"Hey!" a voice boomed from behind the commotion. It was Jel, one of the masters at Ragoon. He was a burly-looking man with an oversized chest that looked too heavy for his short legs. His face was hot red under his thick beard of a similar color, his wavy hair parted severely down the middle. He stomped down the hill from the woods, hard to miss in his red and blue plaid shirt that was neatly tucked into his short blue jeans. He breathlessly circled his subordinates who were almost twice his size in stature, looking Neal right in the eye but not stopping to study what was there. He kicked up a cloud of dirt as he dragged his feet. He took a huge gulp of air and continued, "I want you all to shut up!"

He paused for effect and the men nodded their heads.

"Now," Jel sighed, never quite catching his breath. He crossed his arms over his heaving chest and grinned broadly, exposing his teeth that were a little red around the edges. "Weekly assignments. Line up."

There was an impatient shuffling of feet as the group of men watched each other closely. Every week they were assigned certain areas to patrol and protect. While patrolling, each team was typically given an extra duty, such as brush burning or mending a fence. They worked in teams of two, sometimes willingly but mostly reluctantly. Many of them wanted to keep training. To keep getting stronger.

After keeping them in suspense long enough, Jel reached into the back pocket of his jeans and pulled out a stiff piece of neatly folded paper. He licked his parched lips as he carefully unfolded the paper and cleared his throat. Shogun could see the shadow of the ink on the paper as it tried to sneak a few hints to the anxious students.

"Luke Hartson and Charles Brightman – you boys will take the eastern slopes. Keep an eye out for the horned boars, they're going deeper into the woods now. Well, get going!" Jel shouted at the two men. He continued yelling obscenities until they picked up their bags of supplies and headed east.

Jel glared around at the remaining group. "I won't be accepting any more attitudes like that! Booker Mackenzie! Daniel May! Southwest corner and I want all those brush piles burned by the end of this week!" Jel shouted. Booker and the other man scurried over to their bags and quickly departed without a word.

Team by team, Jel worked his way down the list. Shogun became suspicious of the forest's seemingly uninterested silence as the number of remaining students was reduced and Neal was still there. Shogun and Neal's eyes met as Jel began to smirk.

"Ah, yes. Shogun Saban and Neal Luhrmann. I haven't paired you two for a while. I'm sending you north, to the pines." Jel looked back to his list, folding it now that he was done.

Shogun's jaw began to tighten as he picked up his bag of supplies. He wouldn't let Neal get to him. He'd just take long, deep lungfuls of forest air. But he felt his resolve begin to dissolve as Neal's voice rang through the air.

"Well, what's our assignment? Are you just sending us north to be pals?"

Jel looked up at him. Shogun was expecting an explosion but there was only a calm smoldering. "Just keep an eye on things. That's all."

A smile twitched at the corner of Neal's lips. "Of course." He nodded to Jel in a way that the trees warned was knowing. Still smiling, Neal slung his pack on his shoulder, patting his sword and sliding the sheath to a more comfortable position on his narrow waist. He looked Shogun up and down. "Ready, Saban?"

Neal left without waiting for an answer besides Shogun's displeased expression. He stomped off into the woods at a fast pace. Shogun followed closely behind, pausing only to glance back at Jel. He met Shogun's gaze and what Shogun saw there shook him. Something was wrong. Something was very wrong.

When Shogun turned back around, Neal was gone. The forest had swallowed him and taken him away, just as Neal had asked. But Shogun could ask, too. He let the forest decide the appropriate distance between the two men and it did. Neal was always just a flutter of a bush ahead of Shogun. Just a splash of a river bank beyond his reach. Shogun let himself believe that Neal was gone, blocked only to the back of his mind where the trees gave him periodic updates.

He let the wind guide him north, to where the chilled air frosted everything with an icy dust. The change in the trees was too gradual for even Shogun to notice. And because even the sun changed positions and the rivers twisted anywhere they wanted to go, the wind was the only real guide available, as unpredictable as it was.

Slowly, the trees lost their bulky girth and became leaner in stature. The trees in the north were impatient and claustrophobic. They needed their own personal space and the feeling of air between their layers of limbs. Needles littered the coarse soil and fooled the traveler into thinking he was passing over a giant thatch-roof that was covering something special. The thick cloud cover appeared to thin, waning away to reveal the pale, bluish-white sky that had been behind it all along.

Common sense and years of training told them to stay with the valleys wherever possible, so Neal and Shogun did. It was nearing the end of the afternoon on the third day and the two woodsmen had made good progress by avoiding each other at all costs. They had shared the same bonfire at night, but only to glare at one another over the hot flames that cast shadows beneath their eyes. Neal and Shogun walked on opposite sides of the valley, the crunching of their footsteps meeting in between.

"You know," Neal shouted from the other side of the valley. "As I've been walking all this way, I've begun to suspect something. I do believe you are an idiot." He stooped down to pick up a rock, heaving it hard into the air before him.

Shogun felt his teeth crack as he ground them together hard. He had tried to ignore muttered remarks from Neal throughout the journey. He would pick up an occasional snicker or lewd song that Neal would sing so loudly the trees would have to cover their ears. But now that he was the target of an actual address, Shogun could stay quiet no longer.

"Keep your eyes in front of you," Shogun shouted back.

Neal scoffed as he bent down to pick up another rock, his pace never slowing. "Remain blissful in your naiveté! It will serve you well in the future, I'm sure."

The wind sighed and then there was silence. Shogun fixed his gaze on the mountains around him, capped in snowy brilliance at their highest points. Ahead of him, a large painted forest stretched out across the mountains until the air became too thin to support them. It was a quaint little valley, forgotten between the two grand mountain ranges that commanded most of a traveler's attention. But Shogun could feel the stability of its firmament beneath his feet. He could feel the numerous seasons that had worn this valley down to its very bone.

He looked over at Neal, simmering. Because the truth was, Shogun wasn't sure of the purpose of his presence in the north. Maybe he was naïve. That quick glance of Jel's face had been enough to get Shogun thinking. His steady pace faltered and the trees became silent. There was something in the sky. A thin, pale trail of smoke was curling in its rise through the atmosphere, hesitant and awkward. Wishing to remain unseen. Though Shogun and Neal were not speaking, when Shogun stumbled, Neal felt it too. He turned to Shogun but followed his gaze. He smiled and touched his sword.

"Finally," he whispered, but the trees amplified it because there were no secrets from Shogun.

Shogun felt his stomach twist. In that sweet smelling smoke, he detected life. There were secrets in that smoke and hope of concealment beneath the ancient trees. And this would have been no problem if not for the two men of Ragoon in their midst, hearing and seeing everything. In the back of his mind, Shogun thought he heard soft chants. Whispers for protection. *They were Wood Witches.* Men and women of the forest who wanted to live by the ways of the sea. They were wanderers that had no home and unloved by both sides. They were different. And different was dangerous to some.

Shogun and Neal met in the center of the valley. In the distance, they could see the figures against the firelight, moving around their encampment. Neal dropped his pack of supplies to the ground.

"Make sense now?" Neal whispered, inspecting his sword.

Shogun didn't answer. He was watching the great expanse of pines before him and listening to them. They stood tall and stared back him, protecting the Wood Witches. He looked down at the grass. The wind was blowing away from the camp, urging him to follow in its direction. *Away.*

"We've chased them off before but look at them. Up to their old tricks again. Disgusting," Neal continued. He pointed his sword towards the camp.

"I want nothing to do with this," Shogun declared, turning his shoulder away. The trees didn't offer their protection for the mere sake of concealment. There was always a reason. There was always a thought behind it.

Neal's face contorted. "You can't turn your back on this. You and I are bound to enter that camp."

"And do what?" Shogun said fiercely. "What?"

"They don't belong here," Neal said simply. "A warning should be enough for any reasonable person, shouldn't it?"

"A warning and that is all. Then we return to Ragoon," Shogun ordered, dropping his pack to the ground.

"Of course. Agreed," Neal replied solemnly. The corners of his mouth were trembling. "I have no desire to surround myself with their magic any longer than I have to. Let's go." And then he was gone.

Shogun felt his heart leap in alarm. *Follow him. Quickly.* He removed his axe from his back and entered the thick cluster of pine trees that surrounded the camp. Sap dripped from the trees like dark tears, shed long before any of them arrived. The smell of smoke grew stronger, the spices in its pungent sweetness unknown to Shogun. His heartbeat thumped in his ears, a raging drum summoning his adrenaline. Shogun slowed his pace as he approached the firelight. He pressed against a tree, becoming almost invisible, and held his axe against his chest.

The smoke ascended from a bonfire in the center of the small clearing, its flames a shade a purple. The fire was surrounded by makeshift dwellings with pine-thatched rooves and oak wind chimes in the doorways. There were adults and children gathered there, conducting some sort of ceremony. He knew enough of the Wood Witches and their unending prison sentence, forced to relocate at the hint of any threat. They were peaceful. They were harmless. And they were expendable.

They were almost of the same thread, Shogun and these people. Both a part of the forest, yet different. Even gathered around the glowing fire, the group still looked small in number. Some of them sat and meditated while others stood and fed the fire with their dried branches, whispers, and thoughts. Shogun watched from the edge of the clearing, his presence still masked by the forest's silent cloak. Masking Neal, as well.

It started with a hush. Shogun focused on one of the meditators, feeling his panic from across the yards. He raised his hand and opened his eyes wide, silencing the others gathered. The whispers and chants stopped. Shogun prayed for the wind to mask his heavy breaths, now amplified in the sudden silence. The Wood Witches gathered closer, already helpless. Men, women, children. The tension in Shogun's head was blasting his senses. He repositioned one finger after another on his axe handle, gripping harder and harder with each additional finger. This would be no warning. This was death. He knew what was coming. *Give him strength.*

"You have desecrated these great pines!" Neal's voice boomed from the shadows, so threatening that even Shogun flinched. The Wood Witches cried out and clung to each other, whispering verses of protection.

Shogun watched the group, seemingly terrified beyond response or reaction. He could not see Neal. Sweat gathered on his brow. His axe began to warm in his hand as he felt his heartbeat in his fingertips. With a loud crash, Neal dropped from above. The Wood Witches screamed and split up, stumbling into their homes or the shadows. Neal's sword was fast, as he'd been taught. He slaughtered with one arm and grabbed victims with the other.

"Filthy trash!" he shouted.

Now was the time. Shogun took a deep breath and held his axe in front of him. He froze as the blade began to glow and he saw himself in its reflection. A memory from long ago reawakened within him. The story of it was written across Shogun's face. He had lived in peace for a long time, burying the past deep within him. Now it was resurrecting, sprouting like a tree, branching power from his head to his toes. From his arms to his axe. *Do not fall into that hate. Stop it. Never become a part of it.*

Neal stopped as Shogun walked into the clearing. He paused and met Shogun's determined gaze. The woman he held gasped and cried, her neck raw and bleeding from where Neal had been looking for just the right slice.

"Stop!" Shogun ordered, pointing his axe towards Neal. "Now!"

Neal wiped the blood from his face and scoffed. "Why, you want her?"

"No more!" Shogun's voice reverberated through the clearing. He did not recognize himself. Each tree was a source of more and more power, thousands of years balled into his clenched fist.

Neal raged. He could feel it, too. The trees had taken a side. He was not left alone, but he no longer had their support. Soon, the trees would not recognize him at all. They would be still when he called for them. He had to act soon. He kicked the woman to the ground and she scrambled away to the shadows.

"If you do this, you will bring a storm upon yourself that you will not survive," Neal continued, circling the fire as he wiped his sword clean, visibly trying to calm his heavy breaths.

Shogun felt like he needed no air. He was beyond that, calmer than ever before. He was a million voices. He was a hundred men in one. This was no secret to him any longer. This power and this strength that he felt pulsing through him, it was siphoned into him through the trees around him. Now, Shogun knew. He understood a thousand thoughts he had brushed aside before. He looked down at his axe glowing in his hand. *Now, he knew.*

Neal faltered when he saw Shogun's axe. "These people are predators!" he hissed. "They are whores! Listen and you will hear." He raised his sword towards Shogun. "Listen to the forest, this is what they want!"

"I am listening." Shogun raised his axe. All eyes and hopes and souls watched him.

XIV

THE SISTER MOON

It took her breath away. Literally, every day. The wind was a thief, rushing against her face and pouring down her throat and nostrils, stealing away her very breath. No matter how she covered her face or grasped her throat, her breath belonged to that wind. And there on the sea, it was just her and the wind and the water and its creatures. Opponents yet comrades. Strangers yet kin. Each day she saw a different aspect of the sea's personality. Calm, secretive stillness or raging, ferocious tirades, Madigan was captive to its whims and fancies.

This place was her home. A home, of sorts. If Madigan could call a prison her home. She was a slave to the tides. She watched her sister moon. She knew her wane more than any other stargazer could. Madigan knew the color of the moon's temperament and when to close the shutters and hide from her unnatural light. She knew the moon was a bitter hostess. Trapped, like her, in a world of night.

Madigan visited the sea every day, dutifully. Her father's boat was now her boat and her father's nets were now her nets. The fish that knew her father had grown old and passed down stories to the next generation. Stories of a good man and his daughter who would escape to the sea. Of a man who only took what he needed and was grateful for that, unlike other men of his kind. Of a girl who knew very little yet felt so very much. And this girl was now a woman. And this woman was not yet good, but not yet bad, either.

The fish took care of Madigan and Sara, all while the moon peered down somewhat spitefully, jealous of the way the creatures loved those girls of the sea. She watched them through her veil of clouds, darting in and out. All Madigan needed to do was rise in the morning and walk to the sand and get in the boat and push onto the water. *Go out to the deep and throw your nets,* said the fish. Catch us and let us feel free. Because we have a choice and choice is all any creature can ask for to feel free.

That's all she needed to do, but Madigan still felt pain. The burden of her sudden thrust into adulthood aged her in a strange way. A girl still stuck in an adult's body, longing for the rest of her girlhood and mourning because it had gone away forever. She performed her tasks numbly, all the while peering up at the moon somewhat spitefully, jealous of the way the sky whisked the moon away. Taking her higher and higher with each passing hour until sunrise peeked over the horizon and she could sleep without fear.

In town, the sisters were oddities. Madigan refused to meet eyes with any of those woodsmen, evil to the core. She needed them to survive, but not to live. And for the most part, Madigan and Sara were left alone. There were occasional snickers and awkward moments on the sidewalk. Because the woodsmen did like fish, after all. They needed them for that, as the sea wanted nothing to do with those people of the trees. The fish would turn their nose up at the smell of fir and swim the other way.

Deep in the core of the forest was the Saban house, red with fury. Roland was never seen again. Paddie had become a specter, seen only occasionally in the woods or late at night in town. If he believed his act on May Day would have made him a hero, he was wrong. Instead, he became a symbol of momentary madness. The town blamed him for inciting their hidden rage. It was him, not them. Paddie took his rage and hid it away deep in his red house, festering like a legion. Madigan felt ill at the thought of him. She did not need the elements to feel that.

There were very few fisherfolk left there. The widows and widowers and orphaned children of the murdered fisherfolk left for other places, somewhere void of that sea of bodies. The ghosts rose from the water at night and called for them, misty figures forbidden to leave the choppy waves. The ones that ran left behind homes and moments and memories. Commissioned by the fallen, the wind would search the empty structures violently, howling for their loved ones. Crying out that they were gone.

Madigan saw her father one time. Years ago she dared go down to the beach, on a path lit by the moon. There on the sea, dozens of spirits lingered. Flickering like candlelight, hopeful flames struggling against the wind yet needing it all the same. Madigan called for her father, crying to hear his voice and tell her what to do. He stared at her for a very long time then went away. She returned night after night but he never came back. He never came back.

Now Madigan was a woman. She didn't know her own body. One day she was a girl and the next, a woman. Her hair was very long and very dark and very of its own opinion. It would twist and linger in the air even after the wind had left for the day. One morning in the mirror, Madigan saw her mother looking back. A younger version of her mother, with eyes that matched her father's. It chilled her to the very core, all day on that warm, muggy sea.

Sara had grown older, too. Youthful and blissfully unaware of her changing body. She ran and ran and had not a care about it. Her knowledge of the elements began to grow organically. She began to have her own secret moments with them, interactions that Madigan didn't understand. She saw Henry in her sister, carefree and adventurously exploring everything around her. Madigan didn't understand that. Because for her, the elements had become a partner in survival and that was all.

It was on this morning that Madigan felt special pain. Sara had gone to school. To the school Madigan never had but should have had. The girl who should have gone to school died the day her parents went away. She was stunted by new responsibility. Fish for food. Fish for money. Fish for survival. Was that not what her mother had said? *Survive. No matter what, survive.*

That day on the beach, the air felt different. Smelled different. The haze over the water was heavy and dank. Madigan watched the sea carefully, contemplating whether to enter her boat. She pulled at her cotton pants and removed her thick sweatshirt. She saw no rain. She was sweating and had no reason why. She thought about the empty crates at home, waiting to be filled before tomorrow's market. Madigan pushed out onto the sea. *No matter what, survive.*

It was fall and the old fish were dying. More now than ever, Madigan had to be sure she received proper introductions to the new, young spawn. The old fish would tell them to listen to her story. They had to be familiar with her nets and know their inner weavings, so that one day when it was their time, they would kiss the sea goodbye and come home with her.

Madigan struggled against the choppy water, her nets tangling in the oars and her hair tangling in her face. She cursed the wind and its constant pushing and prodding. The fish were distracted, as though they were having brief moments of clarity and seeing those nets in a different way. Madigan cried out and slammed the oars down to the bottom of the boat.

Then, like a rush of exhaled air, she heard it. Madigan twirled around in the boat, her throat clenching as though she had released the scream herself. Chills of sweat gathered on the back of her neck. If she could have known for sure, she would have sworn she heard her sister scream. Very faint and unreal, as though her sister was in a far corner of Madigan's very mind and shrieked. Sara's scream was undeniable. Madigan had heard it a hundred times, whether in fun or fear.

Again, a scream. An echoing scream, not heard by her ears. Madigan scrambled for the oars. Was it faster to swim or row? Swim or row? *Row. Row fast.* Her eyes welled with tears so that she had to rely on instinct to get back to the shore. *Hold on, Sara.* "Hold on!"

She was almost to the shore when she heard it. A real scream, long and sad. It drove through Madigan's heart like a knife, twisting and diving deeper and deeper. She fell to the floor of the boat, releasing her own scream. She jumped out and stumbled through the water, the waves helping her onto the sand. Madigan ran and ran and ran until she was at her house. She found the front door slightly open.

The wind grabbed her wrist and asked her to hesitate. To prepare herself and breathe. Beyond the door with the seashell knob, Madigan found her naked sister strung from the ceiling. Blood drip, drip, dripped down her legs to the floor. One hand was strained around the noose and the other drooped to her side, palm up. Her body swung in the burst of air, the rope stretching and creaking. Stretching and creaking. Sara's eyes were open, pointed at the sea for one last look before she crossed those waters forever.

The room became a blur. It started with a slow spin, rapidly picking up speed. A sound came from Madigan that was not her own. Pain that her voice could not express so it came deep from her soul instead. The restless spirits beneath the sea stirred, unable to reach above the waves for fear of burning in the sunlight. But they heard her. They recognized her. They rallied for her. The waves became taller and bolder.

One by one, the windows of the little Madigan house exploded. The wind burst through the door, standing in the entryway like a giant warrior, weapon in hand. Howling for vengeance. Madigan's body pulsed with every heartbeat. She was every part of this house and every part of this house was her. The waves roared in her ears. Ocean water filled her lungs yet she could still breathe. The tide pulled at her hair, feeding her thoughts through each tendril. The boards of the house creaked and moaned, generations of memories crying out for justice. *Not their little Sara. Not that little one.*

The elements had caught her eye and Madigan met them. They came closer to her, step by step. Madigan was paralyzed, breathing heavier and heavier, locked in their gaze. She wanted to look away but the things she heard and learned were what she needed and they knew that. They took her back to a night on the beach. A night long ago, cast in the light of the moon. No other souls on the water but her father, a barely recognizable shadow no longer silenced. She could hear him and he told her what to do. Many, many things to do. Then he told her two words. "Never again."

Sara dropped to the ground and Madigan crawled over to her sister, breathless in the dying whirlwind of air. Her tears soaked her sister's soft, silky hair. She covered Sara's naked body, painfully aware of her sister's last moments. Madigan's fingers cracked with static. In the corner, the elements watched her. *We will never be apart, you and I.*

"Never again," Madigan whispered into her sister's hair.

Night fell across the sea. From her mother's dark kitchen sink, Madigan watched the spirits of the fallen rise. She could hear them now, the sad voices of the keep. Madigan buried Sara's body in the front sands of their broken home, as close to the house as she could get. She would one day find her way to the sea, but for now slept safely, nestled in the damp sand. Kept watch by their shell of a house. And Madigan wanted it that way, for a while at least. The sea was about to become a very strange place, indeed.

They were still reacquainting, the elements and Madigan. She leaned on the counter and heard them out, explaining all the unexplained. And slowly, moment by moment, Madigan knew herself again. The girl before the boat and the fish and the death of her parents. She cried and wept and mourned for many, many things. She remembered a hundred moments. She understood a thousand more. Each breath filled her with more life. There in the darkness, they formed a secret pact. The wind shrieked through the house, rattling the cupboards and shaking the unshakeable foundations, following Madigan into the midnight grasses.

XV

THE HOLIDAY TREE

He dreamed of a time in the forest, around the holidays. When the days were short and the nights were long and the dampness ached inside of him. No matter how many layers he wore, that damp dampness could find a hole or a weakness in the thread and sneak through to settle against his skin. Since Paddie and Roland were men of tradition, they held to this steadfastly even when it came to holiday decorations. In years prior, a Holiday Tree would show up at Shogun's house one afternoon and they would make a place for it in their home until the holidays ended. Then the withered tree was dragged outside, leaving its crispy needles behind. A trail of dry teardrops, leading all the way to the door, sad to say goodbye. And they wouldn't disgrace that tree by letting it rot or be slowly consumed by bugs over time. They would slice the tree into honorable pieces and burn it to keep away the chill, that damp dampness. Any tree would hope for an ending like that.

One year, Paddie and Roland asked Shogun to go with them to find their Holiday Tree. Their houseguest of honor that would only stay a few weeks at best. Shogun couldn't believe it. He layered up and they trudged for days through the forest, nodding and greeting each passing tree politely enough. Sometimes a tree would garb itself in wispy mist or douse themselves in the most fragrant aroma to catch their attention, but the men and boy would just continue on. That was not their tree, not yet.

On the third day, they came into a dense gathering of fir. They were sentries, locked together in valiant lines across the land. Ready to stand against whatever came their way to protect their forest. Shogun saw their Holiday Tree first, almost completely hidden behind a burly comrade. The tree was a sensitive sort, out of place in that band of warriors. Dreaming of the sky and other places. When it saw Shogun, it saw home. *Home.* Shogun gently touched its rough exterior but saw what laid within. They smiled at each other and felt such a tenderness towards the other there were no words to say. Paddie and Roland patted him on the shoulder. *Good job, Shogun, you found her.*

Back at home, Shogun and the Holiday Tree spent nights talking by the fire, sharing the few stories they had learned so far. Shadows danced on the walls and they made up tales about the figures they saw. Then Shogun's Holiday Tree told him about the ways of the trees. How they knew things and could share it with him if he only asked properly. Their roots knew the ground and their limbs knew the air, and could reach quite a distance in both directions. So Shogun and the Holiday Tree would practice and soon Shogun didn't need practice, anymore.

The morning of the Holiday Tree's departure was very sad. Shogun cried and cried and it was allowed by Paddie and Roland at the time since he was still a little boy. But the Holiday Tree had no regrets and was grateful for every single second. This is why it had grown from a seed into a beautiful tower, so that one day little Shogun would find it and smile knowingly. It gave Shogun one last brush on the cheek and said goodbye. And Paddie and Roland said how they had never seen a tree give so much heat, last so long, and provide so well in that damp dampness of winter. Hand to the wall, Shogun fell asleep by its warmth every night, permeating through the house like a gentle blanket. There was never another Holiday Tree like Shogun's Holiday Tree. And he always remembered that.

Shogun awoke with a start. He had been sleeping, dreaming of that safe warmth. He was lying in a damp bed of ferns, a layer of dew gathered on his skin. They were trying to keep him warm but accomplishing the opposite effect. The rain poured in steady sheets, more purposeful than usual, dousing him awake. At first, he forgot where he was. Maybe he was just a boy again, lazing off in the woods and lost track of time. Soon Roland would happen across him and chide him back home before Paddie realized he had been gone too long.

But Shogun was no boy. He was a man, now. A man that had killed, just like his father and grandfather, those two men in the mirror. Shogun's hand looked clean and smooth now, but no amount of rain could wash away that memory of Neal's blood. Drip, drip, dripping from his axe blade. There in the firelight, Neal's eyes had lost all spark. No smoldering smoke. No sign of that last, quiet ember. Limp and lifeless, quiet forever. Shogun watched the life flow out of Neal in slow motion. He was that cause. He looked up at the Wood Witches. He was that hero.

The Wood Witches had scattered and ran after Shogun fell Neal. Who were they to know whether Shogun was a rogue killer or simply a man who did good and wanted to stop evil. And Shogun had no idea himself. He had just seen and reacted. He had stepped in and swung. And before he knew it, Neal was on the ground and the Wood Witches were safe.

There was a clash of elements afterwards. Confused whispers and unsure rumblings echoed in his ears. Cheering and cursing. It would not be long until word spread across the mountains and the sleeping Ragoon would awake into a hungry monster. It would start with one cabin. A restless sleep filled with dreams. Until those dreams became stronger and stronger and the inhabitant would wake up from the intensity of it all. And in the fog of the cold window by their bed, they would see Shogun by the firelight and Neal at his side, eyes without a spark. A brother of Ragoon killed by another. They would find him. And they would kill him.

Shogun had run. Not out of fear, but adrenaline pulsing so overwhelmingly that he had to run, run, run to circulate it before it caused his heart to explode. The rain was relentless. It did not hesitate because it was dark or cold or Shogun was dealing with a lot at that moment. It breathed freely and let it all go. So Shogun breathed freely and let it all go. He let the trees guide him through the deep black night and he became a careless spirit, allowing emotions and thoughts to evaporate through him and not leave a single mark. He had run until he could run no more and collapsed to dream his own dreams.

Shogun sat up and backed up against the solid frame of an old tree. He prayed for no breath. He couldn't make a sound. He needed to be stiller than the earliest hour of morning when all creatures were still asleep. But this old tree knew a thing or two about concealment. How else would it have grown so very old. It was so old it could smell the change of seasons and no other tree had a vantage point like him. It peered down on all the young saplings and muttered over their impetuous chatter. *Be quiet, you fools. Your musings are so tiresome. Stand tall and strong like me and we will never fall.* Shogun had chosen a good tree to help him listen.

He listened for a long time, his fingers perched an inch from his axe. Trembling ever so slightly, the old tree noticed. *Breathe, you damn boy, that's not going to help anything.* The tree couldn't hear a thing over that sapling chatter, ridiculous and petty. With a loud rustling it shushed them to silence. The old tree helped Shogun reach across the miles, over the farthest horizon, to Ragoon. To an empty Ragoon. They were gone, looking for Shogun. Seeking vengeance against this traitor who helped the Wood Witches. Who killed the fiercest of them all. And that simply would not do.

Run, boy, run. Shogun needed no further prompting than that. The trees guided him as much as they could without sending too much information into the void. For in that void, anyone with sense could access it and find him even faster. Sun poured through the vista of trees in front of him, blinding him as it reflected off a thousand raindrops, little prisms of the air. Shogun ran towards the light. *Run, boy, run.* He burst through the trees and nearly fell down a deep ravine if not for an obliging fir branch that reached out a limb for Shogun to trip on.

He was out of the deep forest. The rain had eased up a bit now to a misty trickle. A lengthy valley stretched out in front of Shogun, leading to the base of an impressive mountain range. Red, orange, and gold leaves created a grand cape around the hills, preparing them for the eventual snow. For the time when the leaves would fall and the tree limbs would be bare except for a thin veil of moss. That was when the snow would find its way there and lay them to sleep with its thick, downy blanket. And they would sleep a heavy, cold slumber full of dreams of their own.

Down in the grassy valley, a thin road weaved crookedly across the muddy terrain. It appeared to be in very poor condition, as though very rarely traveled and because of this it barely kept up appearances. Why bother. *But keep looking,* the trees suggested. *Don't be swayed by first glances.* Shogun looked closer. His heart leapt. Down on that windy, apathetic road, he saw a sign. It was a bus sign standing next to a wobbly little bench that rocked in the wind.

"It can't be..." Shogun whispered to himself. The trees heard him and winked to each other. He kicked his way free of the fir branch that still had its limbs wrapped around his ankle. Standing tall, Shogun could see a small dot in the distance, moving rapidly down the hill to the valley. It was a bus.

Sliding down the hill, Shogun sputtered in the sprays of mud he left in his wake. He knew very well he was leaving clue after clue for the Ragoon warriors close on his trail. He could sense them on the corners of his mind, a raging storm threatening to strike him down. Lightning and fire flashing through the sky, voices raised in angry unison. It only drove him faster, never looking back.

He finally reached the bottom of the hill, rolling exhausted into the middle of the gravel road. He spit out dirt and breathed in the damp, clean air of the valley floor. Shogun brushed himself off and stood at the bus stop. In the distance, the bus screeched and buzzed and accelerated through the valley, causing deer and other small animals to run for cover. This had obviously happened before. He looked up at the bus stop sign. Etched in the wood were schedule times of a sort. *Spring flower buds. Summer hazy heat. Fall orange leaves. Winter quiet solstice.* He looked around at the fall orange leaves.

The bus rolled to a stop in front of Shogun. The door creaked open and a voice from long ago boomed through the air.

"Well, aren't you just the sorriest looking creature I have ever seen. Don't y'all take baths there in Ragoon?" Meadowsweet hollered.

If Shogun's ears were not ringing from the volume of her voice, he would have thought he was dreaming. He was taken back years ago, to when he was a boy, standing at another bus stop and needing her help. Now he was a man at this bus stop and he needed help whether he wanted to admit it or not.

"Meadowsweet," Shogun said, shaking his head.

Meadowsweet raised an eyebrow. "Obviously, it's me. Whatcha doing out here in this empty wasteland? Whatcha you running from now?" She paused and answered her own question. She looked Shogun up and down. "Ah. No one was taking a bath in Ragoon last night, were they?"

"No." He shook his head. Shogun wasn't sure how much she really knew or how much he should divulge. She did enough talking for both of them, anyway.

A dramatic sigh. "Well, I suppose you'll be needing a ride then, babycakes? A fast ride at that, I'm supposing again. Well, get on! I'm on a schedule, you know!" Meadowsweet winked and a bell rang in the distance, echoing down the valley and bouncing off the mountains.

Shogun jumped on the bus and the door shut behind him. The bus took off, weaving down the valley road again. Shogun watched out the windows and he could have sworn he saw movement in the hills. Had the trees held off Ragoon as long as they could? The trees were tight-lipped and only speaking with their eyes. *Be safe, Shogun.* Meadowsweet picked up the pace, pressing her foot down in a sudden burst of acceleration. Shogun was shaken out of his stare as he stumbled to the floor.

"Why don't you go sit down, sweetums? I'm sure you really haven't had a chance to think. Anyway, I know a few little lovies that are just dying to get reacquainted."

"No, no I haven't..." Shogun's voice trailed off. He felt his knees lose strength and his shoulders seemed heavier than if he were wearing the thickest suit of armor. He stumbled to the middle of the bus, sitting down with a long exhale.

His eyes were drawn upwards. Slowly at first, a trickle of fuzzy light seeped out of a crack in the ceiling. The trickle became a stream and the stream became a fast river, flowing like an unleashed dam of light. Shogun watched the little creatures descend through the air until they reached out and carefully touched his face. The hairs on his face stood on end in anticipation. They could barely believe this was the same Shogun.

"Beautiful, aren't they?" Meadowsweet sighed, watching in the reflection of the rearview mirror. "My little light bulbs, brightening up the most gloomy day. And they know a thing or two, I'd say. Those pretty old souls."

"Do they?" Shogun whispered. He felt the dust sprites crawl across his scalp. Delicate little fingertips tracing letters across his skin. Forming words for him to discover later. They billowed under his damp clothes and nestled near his heart that was thump, thump, thumping. The sound was so comforting to them that they gathered all around it, finding safety in the warmth of his chest. A collective sigh radiated through the dust sprites. Life. Love. Shogun.

There against his skin, they made Shogun a part of them for those moments and he felt what they felt. And they mourned many things. Babies lost. Children left alone. People in pain. Tears at night. Empty homes and howling winds. Confusion and sadness. They felt it all and sometimes it became so overwhelming they had to believe in something brighter. So they would glow and think of each individual heart, beating without malice, just to provide life and love. And above all, they believed in Shogun's heart the most.

Why me, he wondered. They whispered and winked. From where they laid, they could see the very threads of his heart and what he was truly made of. It gave them more hope than ever before. They saw clearly why the trees had chosen him. Why his axe had transformed for him. He had saved a good soul and stopped a bad one. He made a decision that disrupted the flow of pain they grieved so much. And by making that choice, Shogun started down a path that would stop many more moments like that. If he wanted to know why that was why.

They are right, Shogun told himself. When his axe struck down Neal, he felt a power behind his hands that he had never known before. In that moment, he knew he was a true warrior of the forest. And he wanted it again and again and again. It was an addicting rush at his grasp only at that moment, fleeting when Neal's eyes went dark and the task was done.

The dust sprites scattered. They had confirmed what they needed at his chest and now they were pulsing with the energy from his racing heartbeat. They were old souls, long and gray, mindful of many things. If he really wanted to know, they would tell him. Meadowsweet raced faster and faster down the winding road, pressing into the dark hills as the sun set. The trees gathered up the night and masked the bus, safely free of the prying thoughts of Ragoon. No star would shine on them tonight. For Shogun was in the eye of the tempest, caught in a blur of learning. The trees held their breath and listened. *It was time for him to know.*

The dust sprites told him of a myth they knew from a long time ago. Of a place that held secrets that were ancient and could be unlocked when the time was right. A shrine, built on the far edges of their world to hold evil far away. And with it, the answer to stopping all evil as well. The dust sprites reminded Shogun of the things they mourned, growing in number each and every day. They feared the time was coming.

The forest and the sea were strong comrades. They were deep waters and ancient woods from the beginning of time. Over time, it was decided they would choose one of their own to be the strongest. To be the one the others count on. And those two would understand many things, beyond others, beyond themselves at some points. Only together would they find the shrine and set things right. And that would change them. And they would change everything.

The dust sprites looked Shogun right in the eye, deep into the dark well of his pupils. Was he the one chosen by the forest? Beat after beat, his heart had told them so. If he was of the forest, who was of the sea? The dust sprites scuttled up to Shogun's head, searching through each tendril of his hair until they found the pathways of his memory. Shogun gripped the seat in front of him as they sifted through images and thoughts. Easily, they found a little girl of the sea. A little girl who knew very little yet felt so very much.

"Madigan."

XVI

THE RED HOUSE

She had been sitting outside the red house for a long time. It must've been a day at least, Madigan told herself. She remembered the night ending and the morning stretching out its arms, startled to find her crouched only a short distance from the Saban house. Before long, the night was back. A sliver of the moon peeked out from behind the curtain of space. Just her eyes, pondering this new Madigan. But Madigan had no time for her, now. She sat outside the red house and watched for a long, long time.

A part of Madigan felt bad for the house. It was not a color befitting to the old forest around it. It stood out like an angry beacon, warning anyone who came near it. She had memories of that house, good and bad. But never this level of bad. The house held its breath and kept its eyes shut hard, hands over its ears. Sending its thoughts to happier times, away from then and now. The house missed their little Shogun. And it despised every bit of Paddie.

Madigan saw signs of him throughout the day. She would see stirring behind the pulled curtains. Doors would open and shut. Once, he paced in the yard behind the house, but she never actually saw him. She just heard him breathing and the wind told her how horrible it would be on the back of her neck. Every hair on her skin stood at attention for hours. The shadows around the little red house stared on blankly. They were numb to him now, prisoners of his watchful gaze.

The illness in her stomach grew intense, a slow ache that turned over and over into burning nausea. This was part of their pact, the elements and her. They agreed to go along with Madigan but expressed their concerns. This man was no man, anymore. He had allowed the darkness inside him to grow unchecked. What was once a crack was now a deep ravine, twisted and eroding the firmament beneath it. And that was a very dangerous thing.

But Madigan had recognized his smell. Unmistakable, unchanged from years ago. She distinctly remembered standing by her father's side and watching them shake hands, Paddie's stench burning her nostrils. And this same stench had been all over her sister, permeating every crevice and slathered across every inch of her cold skin. So if he thought he would get away with it, Madigan had another idea in mind. The moon peeked out a bit more, intrigued. Putting the pieces together. As jealous as she may have been, she grew hot with the thought of one of those girls being harmed. She burned into Madigan's mind, urging her on. *Never again.*

That night, Paddie knew something. She could tell. He stood in the window, only a silhouette behind the thick curtain, the light from his lantern flickering behind him. A ghost of his own sort, trapped in his own house. Unable to speak as there was no one to hear him. Madigan met his hidden gaze. The elements stirred at their game, uncomfortable in the crossfire. And she continued to wait for a long, long time.

Morning came with a heavy dew, immobilizing any waking life. *Stay asleep,* the elements told them. *Dream of some other place than this.* A snaky mist crept from the woods, slithering around the house and when finding nothing, retreated back to its den. Commissioned by Paddie, Madigan knew. When the mist was gone, she approached the house with careful steps, stiff from lack of movement. The moon faded away, frustrated at the approaching sunlight. *He is sleeping,* she told Madigan with her last breath. Sleeping a restless sleep, aware of the eyes outside his house.

Madigan crept to Shogun's old bedroom window, as she had many times before. She slipped silently against the house, shushing its happy surprise at the sight of her. The window was open. Madigan paused and peeked inside. There was no one in Shogun's room. Climbing through the window, she calmed the startled insects and shadows that had made residence in the long-abandoned room. They said nothing, alerted nothing. *She was there to help them.*

Except Madigan couldn't breathe. She was panicking inside. The elements told her to calm herself and take a breath, they were right there. They had made a pact. And Paddie was going to die. But his stench suffocated her. She felt like she was drowning in it, imagining a sea of putrid, yellow water. She clawed at her neck desperately. He had soaked into every fiber of that building. If she could just catch her breath, she could think. Her heart raced and her mind filled with chatter. The elements began to sound like a call in a distance, echoing further and further away. Fading further and further away, lost in the busy crowd.

The door snapped open and a hand grabbed Madigan by the hair. She choked as Paddie threw her against the wall. She crawled away blindly, in any direction but him. The house was dark, an inky black that was impenetrable. It mourned that she had found her way there. She felt her way into the hallway, tumbling over slimy debris.

"You!" Paddie shrieked from the darkness.

With a burst of air, Paddie was pushed back down the hallway. Madigan heard him tumble head over heels across the hardwood floors. She saw her hand in front of her face, outstretched and trembling. The elements urged her to fight back. *Fight back.* Paddie struggled to his feet heavily. He cursed under his breath and rasped.

A warmth appeared in Madigan's hand. A small flame casting a big light. In it, she saw Paddie's true form, watching her. A black darkness that dripped from his eyes. He charged for Madigan down the hallway and she let the light flicker out, disguising her in darkness again. But this time, it was her darkness.

Paddie tore the room apart, calling and taunting her. "I can smell you! Charlotte…sweet Charlotte…come to me…" he hissed.

Madigan hid on the ground but she began to tremble again and lose focus. Even the elements struggled to hold out against that stench that was years in the making, preparing itself for any intruders. And Madigan was the Queen Intruder of them all. She faltered and Paddie stopped. He laughed loudly. The hairs on Madigan's neck froze. She closed her eyes. She prayed that her sister was still waiting for her, there in her fresh grave. She'd join her soon, she knew it.

"Sweet Charlotte…there you are…"

Paddie reached for her and Madigan could feel just the tip of his fingers brush against her hair. And then he was gone.

The elements shook her and Maddie opened her eyes with a jolt. *She was still there, still alive.* The living room turned over into a mad struggle, two outlines barely visible in the morning light. She backed against the wall and covered her ears, trying to block out the sounds coming from Paddie as he screamed and shouted against his silent attacker. They tumbled into the dining room and the table cracked and split.

Suddenly the house began to glow. Paddie backed up as the silhouette of a man holding an axe became distinguishable. The weapon was glowing. The figure straightened from where he was thrown against the table, his axe pulsing in the thick darkness.

Paddie froze, marveled by the light. "What is this?" he whispered breathlessly, reaching towards it.

The man shook off his shoulders and began to approach Paddie, his axe raised at his side. "I'll show you," he panted.

Paddie turned and stumbled back towards Madigan, reaching out and grabbing her by the collar. She gasped and pushed back at him. One greasy hand was clamped around her neck as the other wrapped around her waist and she felt her feet leave the ground.

"You...first..." he whispered in her ear.

Madigan saw a flash of light and she was released, Paddie crying out as his hand fell to the floor. As she caught her breath and eyes focused, her head began to fill with the whisperings of the house. The calls of the trees outside, rallying for the man standing between her and Paddie. She finally saw his face and her stomach dropped. It was Shogun. Still there, still alive.

Shogun pinned Paddie against the slimy wallpaper with the edge of his axe blade, only a heavy breath away from slicing his throat forever. He met his father's gaze, unflinching as he stared into the blackness he found there.

"How?" Paddie croaked, furiously grasping at the weapon with his long fingernails.

"I came back," Shogun declared. He stood firm as he studied every line and corner of his father's face, searching for anything he recognized. Any glimpse that would stop him from what he was about to do.

"I...just..." Paddie struggled to complete a sentence, sputtering as the axe pressed further and further.

"I know," Shogun whispered coolly. He pressed through until the blade touched the filthy wall. Paddie fell limply to the ground in pieces, his blood clumping to the ridges in the wallpaper. The house stood still, hands covering its mouth in disbelief. *Paddie was dead. Shogun was alive. They were free.*

Shogun stared at the shape of his father on the floor. He had determined it was only a shell, housing something dark that had killed his father long ago. He wiped his axe on the filthy shirt of the figure on the floor then turned away.

Madigan finally caught her breath. She watched Shogun carefully, unsure if this was a dream or reality. The dark blood from Paddie soaked through the floorboards, down to the earth, where it would swallow and bury it forever. The elements watched them both carefully, curious as to how this would unfold. Shogun turned to Madigan and studied her. She was a faint figure in that dark house, but he knew it was her.

"Anyone else here?" Shogun asked her quietly. He gripped his axe, flexing over and over in his waning adrenaline.

Madigan could only shake her head. She couldn't find the strength for words. She looked down at her hands. They were her same hands, her same fingers, her same veins. But inside that house, they had been her wind and her light.

"Stay here." Shogun left back down the hallway, opening doors and looking inside. He paused before turning back, looking one last time at the hallway he had run up and down a thousand times. He knew every creak and crack. The small bit of light through Shogun's open bedroom door filtered into the house. Hesitant at first, but when seeing the coast was clear, turned into a bright out-pouring of sunlight. Shogun looked inside, remembering.

Madigan watched as Shogun came back to the living room. He looked huge from her seat on the floor, a giant axe-wielding tower stomping across the floorboards in his boots. He reached out and pulled Madigan to her feet.

The house began to tremble. A faint shiver that steadily built into a quake. Years of dust filled the already thick air, ashy particles that had grown too big for their own good. The pictures on the walls shook, anxious to explore their chance for freedom. They released and crashed to the floor with ear piercing shatters.

The house was collapsing. His house, melting away. It had held together as long as it could, to trap Paddie and keep him contained. To make him feel safe so he wouldn't wander away. Because it knew what bad things he did when he wandered away. And when the house saw their little Shogun, grown and alive and safe in the outside world, it knew its job was done. A little boy they loved so very much. They kept him safe and helped him run away. They brought him feelings and memories. He may have felt alone, but he never was.

The ceiling began to crack and large chunks dropped through the air like heavy raindrops. Shogun and Madigan ran back into his room, stumbling for the open window which was broken from Shogun's less subtle entry. Many times that window had served as his means of escape and here it was again, providing safe passage.

Once they were outside, Madigan hacked up the crud that had settled and festered in her lungs from the Saban house. Shogun watched the house melt away. A final sigh of relief escaped with the structure's collapse, rising into the air to stretch its wings in glorious freedom. It would soar amongst the clouds and look down at the place it once called home. And with its escape, it freed a thousand memories. They blew past Shogun in a gust of wind, leaving him breathless in their wake.

Madigan watched from behind Shogun, sizing him up. This little boy had grown into a man. *A woodsman.* But he was a woodsman that killed one of his own. That had to mean something. His own father with his own blade. The man that killed her father and brother and sister. The man she couldn't even kill herself. She burned inside, loathing her weakness. But they had made a pact, she and the elements. And one way or another, Paddie had died.

Shogun turned to Madigan. She saw a thousand things in his eyes and it startled her to see a glimpse of herself in his gaze. The woods went very quiet to listen.

"What happened to you?" she whispered. There were tears in her eyes and she didn't know why. Years of questions burning her tear ducts.

"I wasn't there that night. The woods…they kept me here, away from it all. Then I went to Ragoon." Shogun looked over to the patch of woods where he had spent the night of May Day, buried safe in the ground.

"I thought you were dead. I thought he had killed you."

Shogun looked back at the remains of his house. "He would have, eventually." He turned to her. "Did he hurt you?"

Madigan had to laugh. How could she even answer that question. Yes, a million times over, with every breath she took he hurt her. "My sister…" was all she could choke out. She couldn't believe herself, covered in tears. Thank goodness the moon was nowhere in sight to see this.

Shogun closed his eyes. The trees told him the sad tale of what this place had become.

Madigan composed herself. "Why did you come back? How?"

"I came here…on a bus. And I heard you in the house so I -"

"But I never screamed. I couldn't even breathe."

"I still heard you."

Madigan looked at him. The trees urged him on. Shogun had her attention. She just needed him to say the words. But the words felt strange, now. In that bus, with the dust sprites reassuring him, it all made sense. He couldn't give up on it now. This was right.

"You and I…are meant to do something." The words sounded ridiculous.

But she didn't look away. There was no reaction. "What."

"We need to find a place. They told me."

"Who?"

Trust her. "The dust sprites on the bus."

She still hadn't looked away. The wind ruffled his hair. *Go on. Go on.*

Shogun started pacing. "This bus…it's driven by a woman named Meadowsweet. She's the one that helped me get out of here and took me to Ragoon. I had to kill…I had to stop one of my fellow brothers. Then I ran off. To escape Ragoon. And she found me again, somehow. Meadowsweet did. And on this bus are these dust sprites. They told me that you and I are chosen to make things right. I just know that I needed to find you and start there."

"And kill your father?"

Shogun stopped. "It was the right thing to do."

Madigan couldn't deny him that. That's what she had been there to do, after all. She had gone to make things right.

He took Madigan's hand and continued. She looked up at him, startled. "I'm sorry about your family. And my family. And all that has been done. But believe me that this is what we're meant to do."

Madigan took her hand back. "Take me to the bus."

XVII

THE LEADING FLAME

Evening had fallen. Shogun and Madigan were careful in their trek through the woods. *There had been things noticed,* the trees advised. Senses alerted. Eyes turned in their direction. The lazy shadows that surrounded the old Saban house began to realize there was no house at all. They muttered amongst themselves and raised an eyebrow. Something was up.

The moon looked down upon them in all her glory. She had seen a new Madigan and had spent the entire daytime reinventing herself. Fretting over her gown for the evening and taking a million last glances in the mirror before it was finally time for her debut. The wind opened the curtains and revealed the moon in all her splendor, glistening in her own light. The thin night clouds whisked across her face like a veil, allowing her to demurely peek out at just the right moments. The stars held back, afraid of her icy bite if they intruded too early. They knew not to interrupt her moment.

Madigan was not used to these dark woods, they held far too many shadows for her comfort. She had rarely ventured from her safe little home at night, waiting for the breaking line of dawn as her signal to step outside. She worked in the light. Even her grandiose sister of a moon was the light in the darkness.

Shogun took Madigan back to the bus stop where Meadow-sweet had delivered him not long before. Music blasted through the evening air, even with all the doors on the bus shut. Through the windows, the inside of the vehicle looked thick with fog or smoke. Shogun knocked on the bus door loudly. Madigan stopped beneath the bus stop sign and waited.

The door popped open with a burst of volume. Meadow-sweet sat in the driver's seat with her short legs propped up on the oversized steering wheel.

"Sugar Plum!" she exclaimed over the music. "What are you doing back?"

Shogun stepped aside and revealed Madigan behind him. The music volume dropped as though some of the notes had died out and left only the beating bass. Meadowsweet slowly lowered her legs and peered across at Madigan.

"Well, well, well. I didn't see this one coming."

Shogun motioned for Madigan. "This is Charlotte Madigan. I need to bring her on the bus."

Meadowsweet paused. "We're busy," she replied with a toothy grin. "Can't you hear this music? The dust sprites are having a little get-together. And she's not invited." She reached for the lever to close the door.

"Now," Shogun insisted, forcing the door open.

"Oh, well then, please, by all means," Meadowsweet replied with a heavy drawl, standing up to bow as Madigan stepped onto the bus, looking her up and down levelly. She turned back to Shogun and sat down in her seat with a huff. "Look who's suddenly gotten bossy."

Madigan ignored Meadowsweet as she walked by, enraptured by the sight in front of her. Thousands of dust sprites puffed through the air with pulsing light. They hadn't noticed her yet. They were twirling through the air with their eyes closed, arms outstretched. Lost in their thoughts and the steady pace of the music. The elements watched through the windows, pressed up to the milky glass. This was not seen often. Wise little dust sprites were usually hidden from sight, carefully accessing each situation. Now they were twirling with abandon, lost blissfully in the air.

Then slowly, one by one, they began to notice her. Even before they opened their eyes they knew she was there, a smile creeping across their mouth with each realization. They approached her slowly, careful not to frighten her with their electric touch. Madigan walked straight into their frenzy, they were so magnetic she had to be with them. To know them. To feel them.

They told her many things. Things that they had told Shogun but some things just for her. They touched a tender part of her that was buried deep within. They knew she was new to this. They knew her strength surprised her. They saw that moment in the dark house, where she had filled herself with light. *Embrace it. Allow it. Listen to it.*

One by one, the dust sprites began to return home, tip-toeing back through the crack in the roof, ready for sleep. They had seen what they needed to see. Madigan felt each and every one of them leave her until she was left with one last dust sprite. It hesitated on her fingertip, reluctant to leave. She held it up in front of her eyes. It saw a vulnerability in Madigan that it could not abandon. Maybe this was its purpose. Maybe this was its path. And it was willing to find out. The dust sprite waved farewell to the others who had been watching from the crack in the ceiling. They smiled and disappeared into the darkness.

Shogun watched as the last dust sprite floated through the air and nestled into Madigan's hair. Her hair that had a life of its own was a perfect home for the little dust sprite. It sunk into her locks and faded, camouflaged in her wiry strands. Madigan touched her hair carefully. She could feel the dust sprite yet she couldn't. She looked at Shogun with new eyes.

"Well, I'll be…" Meadowsweet whispered.

A gust of wind rattled through the open bus door. It was cold, leaving frozen fingerprints along the thick glass. The luggage compartments vibrated and popped open as random items fell through the air like rain.

"Well, that's my cue!" Meadowsweet shouted, clamoring around the bus as she closed compartments and wiped off windows. She stumbled up to the glove box until she pulled out a tightly wrapped coat. It burst open with a pop and she quickly zipped it over her body. "Time for you to leave, honey kin! Gotta get to my next stop!" She jumped in her driver's seat and motioned towards the open door. "And that means you too, Miss Charlotte Madigan."

"Leave? Aren't you taking us with you?" Shogun protested as Madigan rushed past him. Once outside, she shook the frost from her clothes.

Meadowsweet sighed. She reached out and touched a gloved hand to Shogun's hair. "Darlin', please. I think I've done enough, don't you? And your little companion there took one of my precious dust sprites, so I think you're making out just fine."

"Shogun!" Madigan whispered sharply from the bus stop.

Meadowsweet rolled her eyes heavily and sighed. "Oh sweetums, your little girlfriend is calling you. She already has quite the leash on you. My stars!"

"Thank you," Shogun said, holding out his hand. "For everything."

Meadowsweet smiled and took his hand. She blinked her eyes at him and bells rang furiously in the distance. "Now, you just have me enchanted." She turned and gripped the steering wheel. "But you better get off this bus before I leave your sea witch in the dust and she melts away. Go on!"

Shogun jumped off the bus and the door shut instantly. The bus burst to a start towards its next destination, taillights trailing in the distance until there was nothing at all. He and Madigan were left in complete darkness. The moon was off behind the tree line, making another outfit change. Their breath was heavy in the silent night. This night that stood still to watch them begin. The ocean prayed and sent their whispers out into the air, carried by the wind. The trees closed their eyes and wished.

"Do you think it really exists?" Madigan whispered. "A place like that?" Her mind raced with the things shown to her by the dust sprites. Her skin tingled with their remaining impressions. This felt bigger than her, so enormous to process she didn't even know where to begin. The dust sprite stirred in her hair, listening.

"More than anything," Shogun answered, watching the last of the dust kicked up by the bus fade away. "It has to."

Slowly, a light began to burn in Madigan's hand. A gentle fire, cool to the touch. Shogun approached and watched, his eyes growing larger with each lick of the flame. Even the dust sprite peeked out from Madigan's hair to watch.

"Lead us there..." Madigan asked quietly. The little flame floated from her palm and caught a ride on the wind, allowing itself to be whisked off in the intended direction.

Madigan looked at Shogun. "Did you have another idea?"

Shogun faltered but shook his head. "No. No, let's go." He took off in the direction of the flame.

Madigan pulled her hair up in a bun to keep the little dust sprite safe and secure. She heard the sea calling for her over the long, midnight grasses. The moon peeked over the tree line, glowing milky white against the black sky. She raised her eyebrows in a question.

"Watch over our sister," Madigan whispered.

XVIII

THE WESTERN COASTLINE

Madigan's flame flew far down the Western Coastline. It always stayed a day ahead of them so that Madigan and Shogun could only see its blazing light at night. A steady beacon in the distance, urging them to follow. It flickered so they knew it was her flame instead of a low-lying star or a lighthouse spotlight. Always in their line of sight, lulling them to sleep like a fireside in the sky.

The rain poured on them and reminded Madigan and Shogun that their progress was too slow. It drained from the sky, weighing down their clothes and bags full of provisions taken from Madigan's house. They had stopped there one last time, the flame waiting for them on the horizon. *Prepare yourself,* it seemed to say. Madigan had no problem stripping everything of value from the house. She knew it was now doomed to the wind's winding moan. It would become a barren shell slowly over time as the wind took a piece away with each visit. It would wear away at the bones of the house until one day it became driftwood on the sand. And the driftwood would roll into the sea and float away for another day. Another time. Another life.

The craggy coastline full of soft sand and hard edges also contributed to the tediousness. The forest was preoccupied as the late fall trees were transitioning into winter versions of themselves, scattering leaves on the earthen floor. Shedding into mossy skeletons, bracing themselves for the winter chill. They passed no one along the coastline. The sea was large and angry and most people could sense it. Best not to investigate, just stay away. A tempest of many built up thoughts. Madigan avoided looking in its direction from beneath the hood of her jacket. Its glowing eyes sent a paralyzing chill up her spine. It churned and grumbled from deep depths below, stirring its creatures into a frenzy. It was raging and calling Madigan to rage along with it.

"We're not moving fast enough," Shogun admitted one night. It was a particularly windy night that tested their patience. He looked huge next to the fire, his shadow sitting atop his shoulders. There was no rain that night, just howling wind that whipped his hair to stand on end. He looked back down at Madigan's flame in the distance, as he did every night, over and over again. Sometimes late at night, when Shogun thought Madigan was asleep, she would see him standing on the dark sand, watching the flame. Making sure it didn't leave without him. "This coast stretches forever. We need a vehicle."

Madigan shrugged her shoulders. Sometimes she wondered if Shogun thought she could whip anything out of sand and wind and fire and water. Maybe he dreamed up in his head a chariot of wet sand, drawn by horses of fire. They would leave a trail of burning embers and ashy leaves as they flew down the coastline, in hot pursuit of that faraway flame.

"Then let's steal something," Madigan replied with another shrug of her shoulders. She pulled her hood over her head a little further. The dust sprite was feeling a bit of a chill.

"Steal?" Shogun balked. "We don't steal."

"Borrow?"

Shogun hesitated. "Borrow is better," he finally admitted.

The sun rose the next morning to a calmer sea. A lazy sea, sleeping late after a night of hellion and mischievous antics. When Madigan awoke, Shogun was packing up their camp but left her breakfast neatly arranged in front of her. He watched the flame in the distance as he rolled up his sleeping bag. One last look before daylight took over. He had to remember its exact location so he could compare it that night and every night after.

"The dust sprite…" Madigan whispered, patting her hair. She shook her hair madly and examined the length of each strand. Her sleepy eyes were now wide awake. "The dust sprite is gone!" She began to shake out her sleeping bag and her clothes.

"Maybe it went home," Shogun suggested. He didn't quite see the purpose of the dust sprite at this point. At this point where he and she knew what they were doing. For the most part.

"No. No, it's staying with me. It told me it would stay with me," Madigan reassured herself, tearing apart Shogun's neatly packed camp. He sighed deeply and began packing it again.

Madigan looked to the forest behind them. A bony forest stood nearby sleepily, not contributing much other than a lazy leaf fall. Shogun paid them no attention, he knew how disconnected the trees by the sea could be. Stuck in limbo between two worlds so they chose apathy instead of a side. Madigan ran off in the direction of the trees, tearing through the deep layers of crunchy leaves.

"We need to go!" Madigan heard Shogun yell after her. But she wasn't leaving without it.

As she broke through the trees she came upon a house. A muted brown house, good at blending in as it had been for some time now. Madigan stopped and ran back to the cover of the trees. There was no light through the old windows. They appeared misty with built up condensation that had made a lengthy home there. The driveway was covered with slick leaves, decomposed after many damp days. The house was abandoned, the elements told her. It had long ago lost its soul.

"Dust sprite!" Madigan whispered loudly. She didn't know what else to call it. She didn't know why she was whispering. But there could be others watching from the woods, through the cover of trees, as well.

Next to the house was a decrepit shed. One door was gone and the other beat lazily against the building. A slow, dying heartbeat, continuing on only because of the passing wind. In the dark shed, Madigan saw her dust sprite. A little orb of light glistening in the thick black.

"What are you doing in here?" Madigan whispered sharply. The shed was thick with old musty smells. She could taste it on her tongue and it made her gag. Old memories that had melted into slush, attempting to bring the shed down along with it. The dust sprite was underneath an old blue tarp, pulsing hard. Madigan held her breath and whisked the tarp away. It flew off with a flurry, escaping into the fresh air and another adventure.

The dust sprite was hovering on the steering wheel of a small sand buggy. It liked steering wheels, it reminded it of Meadowsweet. It nestled its face all over the steering wheel and sighed.

"Good job!" Madigan exclaimed as she brushed off the years of built up dirt and sand. The keys were in the ignition, as was not strange for a sand buggy. Her family had once owned one, meant for quick excursions that could waste no time searching for missing keys. She touched the cool metal and smiled. The dust sprite returned to her hair and smiled too, reliving those memories with Madigan.

Shogun heard the sound of a motor in the distance. The trees all turned in that direction, startled from their restful slumber. A rush of air passed them, a windstorm without wind. Madigan emerged through the tree line driving a dirty sand buggy, painted the color of sand and likely running on sand as well. It was loud and obnoxious but on that beach with no one there, no one cared.

"Borrowing it?" Shogun asked above the engine noise.

Madigan turned off the sand buggy. She slammed an extra gallon of gas in front of Shogun. She felt breathless and exhilarated.

"The dust sprite found it," she explained. Anything the dust sprite did had to be right, anyway.

As soon as the bags were tied to the lightweight sand buggy, they were off. The tires were designed for the slippery miles of sand littered with hidden stony crags and splintery driftwood. The dust sprite remained perched on top of the steering wheel, pointing in the direction of the faraway flame. It was a two-seat sand buggy and Shogun wanted to try his hand at driving this invention of the fisherfolk. Madigan looked behind them. Through the dissipating dust, a dark storm cloud was billowing in the afternoon light. Rearing like a monster, ready to unleash its minions. Shogun saw it too, in the reflection of his side mirrors. Darker than a cloud should be. He pushed the sand buggy on faster, racing towards the warmth of the leading flame. Maybe it was nothing. But maybe it was something.

The topography of the beach began to change. Madigan observed it and felt hollow. A place she thought she knew so well apparently had many different sides. Through his travels, Shogun had seen how the trees had many distant relatives, differing in spacing and color and reaction to the seasons. But Madigan did not know the beach could change from cliffs to smooth sand, from mountains that erupted through the waters to mountains that were far away shadows. She wondered if the creatures of the deep were different as well. Did the stories from the fish near her little home reach this far?

Nights later, Shogun watched Madigan walk into the sea. A warmer sea on warmer night with a thousand stars to light her way, interested in this little creature of the sand trying to take on those choppy waters. It had been a day since they'd eaten and Madigan had known what to do. Shogun watched and wondered why she whispered to those wild waves. He understood a part of it because he knew the stirring inside when he places his hand on an ancient tree. A tree whose veins throbbed with knowledge that he could sit and lean against and learn from forever, until one day he melts into a pile of bones. But the sea was strange to him and it was even stranger that Madigan could emerge from the waters with an armful of fish. She would not talk the rest of that night, keeping herself and her thoughts beside the fire.

"Are we getting any closer?" Madigan asked the next morning. She was awake before Shogun. "Do you think we're the only ones who can see the flame? What if others are following it?" She felt sudden anxiety about that distant burning ball.

Shogun stirred and kicked off his sleeping bag. He needed layers upon layers to keep out that damp chill of the nearby salt water. "You're the one who created it, don't you know?"

"No," Madigan balked. "I didn't create the flame. It's a flame." Shogun's eyes lit up as she handed him a cup of strong coffee.

When Madigan turned back the flame was gone, disappeared without even a pillar of smoke in its wake. Her heart skipped several beats and the dust sprite came out from her braid to take a look for itself. It had felt the rush of adrenaline pulse beneath her skin like an undercurrent. Madigan struggled for words and just pointed in the direction of that forever stretching beach, now flameless.

Shogun studied the horizon for several moments carefully, taking slow and deliberate sips of his coffee. The morning ocean mist had settled in his hair thickly, trying to figure out the mind of his forest man. "I had a feeling that would happen," he said finally, wiping the water out of his hair. The mist would have to try again tonight.

"You did?" Madigan asked sharply.

Shogun began packing up the camp slowly, being careful not to spill a single drop of his coffee. "You started talking about it like it wasn't really yours. Of course the flame would disappear, you stopped believing in it."

"But I did believe in it! I haven't doubted for a minute!"

Shogun looked back at the empty horizon. "Well, you must have a doubted for a second, it's still gone." He glanced up at the trees who rolled their eyes. *She was still a bit of an amateur.* Not like their Shogun.

"Doesn't matter," he added, finally putting away the dry coffee cup. "We've got to keep going. Pack up."

"But the sand buggy, it's out of gas."

"So we walk like before."

Madigan paced. The dust sprite tried to calm her down by hovering next to her temples, whispering soft thoughts, hoping to distract her from the frustration quickly building inside of her. But it was just a whisper in a giant windstorm and it was lost to Madigan. So many days. So many nights. Following that flame. She had believed in it. It wouldn't just abandon her for no reason.

"No...no," Madigan said quietly. She closed her eyes and felt the flame over the miles, still burning for them. Still their light in the distance, warm to their faraway touch. *Don't give up on it,* the flame pleaded to Madigan. She had asked it to lead them and it was leading them where they needed to go.

"It's still there!" she blurted out, turning back to the empty horizon. She exhaled as she saw the flame's misty outline, just barely visible against the thick clouds. It had camouflaged itself in response to Madigan's fear of being followed. She laughed and felt herself start to tear up at the same time. "It's still there."

Shogun glanced back at the trees with an arch of his eyebrow. They crossed their arms and looked away. *Maybe she isn't such an amateur, after all.* Madigan scrambled around and quickly packed up her bag. The dust sprite struggled to hold on.

"Let's go!" Madigan shouted, running off in the direction of the flame. Now that she had her sights on it, she wasn't letting it go again. Shogun ran after her, giving one last pat to the sand buggy they were leaving behind. He was beginning to understand this beach and this sea. He knew that eventually the wind would cover the sand buggy in mountains of sand. Then the wind would take the sand away until it revealed the sand buggy to another traveler one day. And the sea would tell the traveler nothing of Madigan and Shogun. Always silently watching. Always swirling and thinking deep down in its depths. Always winding and whispering.

XIX

THE SOUTHERN LAKES

W*ake up.*

Shogun opened one eye. Very slightly, so that he could get the faintest sense of his surroundings. It was still night, quiet in the very early morning hours before dawn. Madigan's sleepy breathing was as steady as a ticking clock beside him. In and out, in and out, never missing a beat in that cloak of darkness, trusting the safety of her sleep. The dust sprite was a dull glow in the soft strands of Madigan's hair, pulsing slow, calming light. The trees rustled in the windless air. Rustling words to him, meant for Shogun's mind only. He didn't need to move his hand to feel his axe blade beneath his sleeping bag. His constant companion, hard as his bones and just as vital to his survival. He cared for that axe better than for his own body. Because without it, there were many times he would not have had a body left.

The long grasses called out to him and the hair stood up on his arms and legs. A strange song that he could not fully identify but knew enough to be wary. Shogun and Madigan had begun to steer away from the sea, steadfastly following the outline of the leading flame. It was easiest to see in the first morning light when the rays of the sun were haphazard, catching it off guard. Day by day, Shogun and Madigan had inched further and further away from the wild sea, into the long grasses of the Southern Lakes. It was a place they knew only from stories and had never seen. A place of shallow, marshy waters and sparse valleys of trees. Of tall skies and giant mountain ranges far, far away from sight. They knew very little of the people who lived there. Or the creatures that slithered beneath the thick waters.

The trees were different there, thin and tall and easily swayed by the wind. Not solid in a storm like Shogun and Madigan's home. Those trees were built strong after defending themselves against thousands of years of ocean winds bearing down on them, trying to wear them away. Year by year they would grow stronger as ancients fell and passed their knowledge onto their decedents. *Stay strong against the gale force. Take deep root and wear the heavy rains like a cloak of dew.* But the trees of the Southern Lakes still did their job. And in their whispers, Shogun heard what he needed to hear. In this land he knew nothing of, he now knew something.

Their camp was dark, the once warm flames having dissipated into drowsy embers just like Madigan. Even with that large expanse of sky, there were hardly any stars causing barely any light. But he could see the dark outlines standing in the nearby gathering of trees, their anxious pacing a dead giveaway. The trees stood still and rigid in their presence. Holding their breath.

Slowly, Shogun gripped his axe and stood up. He had learned from Ragoon that there was no point in surprising your opponent. An aggressive opponent would meet you head on and a passive opponent would run at your show of strength. He wanted them to see his own outline. The sharp and pointed blade of his axe, unrecognizable yet unmistakable. Slowly, he felt the adrenaline ramp up through his bloodstream. First a trickle, then a full on raging waterfall, sweeping him along with it. He had to focus his breathing to calm every reflex tensing to react. The dark outlines met his gaze and stopped pacing. Then they were gone. So they were passive opponents. And like passive opponents, they would be back. And they would slowly grow bolder until one day they were passive no more.

The next morning came with a bitter wind. It ran across the flat marshes with bursts of energy, whipping the grasses this way and that. It was exhilarating and burned the lungs at the same time. When Madigan awoke, her face was red from the wind's chill. The morning light beamed down on them with no mountains to break its bold rays. It was free to rise and burn with no barriers in its way. Madigan covered her eyes with her hair and moaned. She was used to the dull, diffused morning light of her home. Not this unhindered blazing fireball.

Shogun stirred the campfire for the smallest bit of heat, his coat pulled over his shoulders as high as it could. Behind him, mist burned from the waking waters of the marshlands that stretched for miles. Hissing into the air, unleashed by the warmth of the sun. Madigan had to study Shogun for a moment, he looked different to her in this light. A secret moment where he did not know she was watching him. Sometimes he still looked like a boy and sometimes he looked like a man. She wasn't sure what this moment was, for he looked a bit of both. Piling the embers on top of each other to make a wall while an axe laid at his side. He caught her watching him and Madigan sat up with a stretch.

"It's getting colder," she yawned. She layered her hair on top of her head so the dust sprite would have all the warm layers it needed.

"I know." It had been a long night and morning for Shogun. He could not go back to sleep after the dark figures left their camp. His adrenaline needed release so he spent the dawn wielding his axe, swinging it through the tall grasses. They snapped instantly at the edge of his blade. Shogun watched the sun rise, breathlessly chop, chop, chopping away at the thick grass until that orb had risen completely.

He had watched Madigan sleep. One minute at a time, the sun rays had crept slowly towards her peaceful face. Peacefulness he never saw as she walked and talked and stood awake. He wondered why but then he didn't. She would clench and unclench her fists periodically throughout her sleep, as though she was rowing through waves of fitful dreams, only to come out the other side with some sort of clarity. Shogun remembered her as a little girl, a child of the sea whose eyes shone bright. Now she was a beautiful yet troubled woman, her eyes swirling with clouds dense with dark rain. Restless in everything but her heavy sleep. And that was why Shogun decided not to tell her of their visitors from the night. He decided it was the right thing to do. He couldn't threaten those precious moments of peace she felt for just those few hours at night.

That day was long. Even in those shortened autumn days, the hours were slow in that place. The shadows stretched long and strange underneath the oppressive expanse of blue sky. The days were getting colder and the wet marshlands gnawed at Shogun and Madigan's skin, numbing them through their thick boots. The relentless dampness even got to Madigan, she who had spent her waking hours floating atop the endless sea. All the while, that flame urged them forward and onward. *Forward and onward.*

"I need to stop," Madigan gasped, stumbling into a thick patch of especially spiky marsh grass. The grass had to be hardy there, building an armor of waterproof scales to shield itself from constant submersion. It was afternoon and Madigan didn't care that her pants were now wet. Her legs ached to the point they were no longer her own. They belonged to pain and pain alone. She dropped her bag in her lap and breathed deeply, suddenly feeling as though air was escaping her altogether.

Shogun stopped as well. He had been leading in front, testing the waters in front of him carefully with each step. He didn't trust this place for a second. He imagined great chasms beneath the water suddenly appearing without warning, sucking him down into their dark, cold depths. He could swim, but maybe not that well. He wasn't willing to find out. Shogun looked up at the blank, blue sky. The air was ringing with heat, even though there was no heat. It was a strange place. There were no trees for miles, far from his sight and hearing. They spoke to him in a low, indistinct murmur.

The dust sprite slowly floated out from Madigan's hair and whizzed past Shogun to scout the path ahead of them. It would do this occasionally, usually coming back with nothing to report and settling back to sleep in Madigan's hair. Dust sprites required a lot of sleep, Shogun observed. But it seemed to be a trusted companion to Madigan, lulling her to sleep and understanding her disguised tears. If anything it was just another set of eyes. And dust sprite eyes were rare to come by.

"I'm so tired. So tired," Madigan whispered, to herself and Shogun and anything else listening. The wind pushed her hair out of her sweaty face and patted her shoulders.

"We can't stop here, we need to find dry ground. I'm not sleeping in this blasted water," Shogun replied, kicking the marsh to make his point.

Suddenly, the murmurs grew louder. Frantic. The trees used their roots to send a message through the soil beneath the water, rumbling across the tectonic plates. *Listen to them*. Madigan's eyes grew wide and he swung around. The dust sprite was careening across the marshy water, under hot pursuit.

Behind it thundered a large creature, swiftly maneuvering through the water as it stomped across the marshland. It towered hundreds of feet in the air, an archway of rushing water pulsing through the creature like a stream of blood. A deep and guttural yell came from its mouth, a cavernous hole that swirled like a whirlpool. Where there should have been eyes were dark slits, surrounded by long tentacles of water.

Shogun instinctively raised his axe. This creature was obviously made of water so he could only hope the force of his blade would break something, anything. Before he could blink the creature was upon them. It stopped and swept a giant wave towards Shogun and Madigan, bellowing along with it.

"Hold on!" Shogun shouted, crouching to the ground. He braced for the impact of the wave but never felt a drop. He could hear the water rushing around him as though he was standing underneath a waterfall. For a moment, he thought for sure he had drowned. When he opened his eyes, he found himself within a giant air bubble, surrounded by a shield of water. Behind him, Madigan was still sitting on the ground with her hands over her ears, shaking and whispering to herself. The dust sprite flew around inside their little air bubble frantically. Outside, the creature paced back and forth, shouting and sending stronger and stronger waves of water and debris.

"Are you doing that?" Shogun shouted over the deafening water, crawling on his belly over to Madigan. It was dark and murky within their bubble and he could barely see from one end to the other. She nodded and kept whispering to herself, afraid to break her concentration.

Suddenly, the creature's hand broke through the water barrier and grabbed for Shogun. It was made of this water, too. It grasped blindly for someone, anything. Shogun swung his axe in vain at the creature and rolled away. He sputtered through the grasses, clawing to the other end of the dark air bubble.

"No!" he shouted as the creature grabbed him finally, dragging him through the thick barrier of water. He was soaked through instantly at the creature's liquid touch. When he passed through Madigan's wall of water, he thought for sure he would collapse under its pressure. There was no air, just the strongest stream of water he'd ever experienced. He could hear Madigan's whispers within its waves. Conjuring it. Creating it. Controlling it.

Finally, the creature swung him outside the air bubble and through the air, still holding onto him with its fluid grip. Shogun's stomach turned upside down and sour as the bright light of the Southern Lakes swirled around him. He had lost his axe somewhere in his passage through the shield of the air bubble. His bones had left him. Now he was a rag doll in the hands of that creature. After several swings, the creature had enough of beating him around and drew Shogun up towards its face. As his eyes settled, Shogun could see within the pit of its mouth, the swirling darkness he had imagined was beneath their feet all along. He squirmed to try to free himself from the creature's grip but only managed to sink deeper and deeper into its suffocating grasp.

Then everything went silent. Again, Shogun assumed he had drowned. The last time he had heard silence like that was when he fell into a river near his house as a child before he knew how to swim. He had sunk very deep, down beneath the current to where the water took on a paralyzing chill. A death chill, he imagined. Before his grandfather had pulled him out, Shogun took note of that silence.

Faintly, he heard a whisper very far in the dark distance. It was Madigan, telling the water what to do. Shogun was dropped to the ground and he immediately sat up above the surface of the water to inhale blessed air. Madigan stood beside him, one hand raised towards the water creature that was now locked in her gaze. The dust sprite swirled around her head like a halo, whipping up a windstorm of hair.

"Quiet, now..." she murmured, keeping her hand outstretched. The creature stopped and slowly closed its mouth. It was mesmerized. From the west, a wind raced across the marshes. It had traveled a long way from the sea, but not too far as it still knew its way around. Slowly the wind built into a swirling storm, dismantling the creature piece by piece. Drop by drop. The wind whipped back around, returning back where it came from. It would introduce each droplet to the tumultuous sea. Madigan thought this creature was better suited there, anyway.

Finally, there was not a single drop left of the creature. Calm restored to the marshland waters. Madigan slowly lowered her hand that was now visibly trembling. She breathed deeply, as though she had been holding her breath the entire time. She turned to kneel down next to Shogun.

"I'm sorry...it took me awhile," Madigan stammered.

"No, you've got nothing to be sorry about. That was amazing," Shogun replied, standing up. "Now me...I've lost my axe. Now that's a problem." He began to wring the water from his clothes. He gave up and began sifting through the grasses, hoping to find his bones laying somewhere within them. He turned back to Madigan. "I don't suppose that's something you can help with, is it?"

Madigan wrinkled her nose. "No." She wanted nothing to do with that nasty weapon of old steel. No matter how many times Shogun polished it, that blade still had the stain of old blood on it. That blade of too many memories, all violent and hard. Shogun's dark and necessary companion.

The dust sprite whizzed past Shogun and drew his attention. Only steps away was his axe, lying still beneath the waters. Suspended in a sort of limbo, aware of its strange surroundings but unsure how to react. When Shogun found it, the axe was whole again. Shogun inspected it carefully and returned the weapon to his back, now complete. The dust sprite nestled again into Madigan's wet hair. It didn't care that her hair was wet, it was time for sleep after that mess. But slowly, the dust sprite rose again. It floated above Madigan's head and hovered there, remaining very still. Madigan followed its gaze.

"What is it?" Shogun asked, peering across the endless marshland. He saw nothing out of the ordinary. No more creatures. No more tidal waves of water. But then again, the trees were too far to hear and the grasses whispered a language he couldn't translate. He was trusting on Madigan here.

"There's someone there," she whispered, motionless. She was straining not to blink, afraid the person she distinguished in the tall grasses would disappear from sight. It was an outline of a man, slowly standing up in the place the creature had collapsed. Chills ran up her neck. She hadn't sensed him. She hadn't sensed anyone in those layers of water. Her mind had reached every droplet and she hadn't sensed so much as a heartbeat. He stood up tall and stared back at them.

Madigan had barely breathed the words and Shogun took off after the man. His axe burned hot on his back as he pushed through the thick grasses. He reached back for it and chopped his way through, allowing him to run fast, fast, faster. The man ahead of him had turned and began to flee, looking back over his shoulder occasionally. This was just a man. Made of bones and blood. Shogun could hear his accelerated breathing. His labored splashes through the water. This was tangible. This Shogun could handle.

The grasses gave way to a deep expanse of water, one of the many Southern Lakes of that territory. It appeared suddenly and did not cause the man to hesitate, as he dove into the water and swam at a fast pace across its still surface. Light was fading and dark shadows were stretching across the water, remaining in the man's wake as he made swift progress across the lake until he disappeared. Shogun stopped at the water's edge and shouted. There was no way he was catching up with his fleeing opponent now. One tall, lone tree watched from the beach. It agreed with him and went back to lazily drinking water.

Madigan finally caught up with Shogun, who was buckled over as he tried to catch his breath.

"Lost him," he panted, shaking his head.

Madigan dropped the soaking wet bags of supplies on the beach. The dust sprite emerged from where it had been leading her through the grasses. She looked from Shogun to across the lake.

"There's nothing we can do now. We need to rest," she said, half to herself. The fatigue she felt had now completely taken over both her body and mind, her soul drained to the last drop. She unrolled her sleeping bag and crawled inside, still soaking wet. "Tomorrow..." she whispered before drifting off to sleep.

Shogun paced around the edge of the lake. It was nearing sunset now, he hated how the light quickly arrived and disappeared in that place. It had just been morning then afternoon and now it was night. There was never a chance to watch and listen and think. He grabbed the bags and began setting up camp near the lone tree. More than anything, he just needed to think.

XX

THE DREAMING TREE

Shogun spent the night leaning up against the old lazy tree, watching Madigan catch her precious hours of deep peace until he drifted off into his own sleep. Shogun dreamed about the old tree and how it had spent most of its years alone with that mute lake. It would get the occasional passerby that came to the lake for water or a swim or an attempt to fish but for the most part, the tree was left to itself. So it grew from a seed to a tree and became lazy and slow, passing time in strange intervals.

And because it had nothing else to do, the tree would watch things. One day a man appeared. This man was different than the nearby villagers who frequented the lake. He would leave and return, studying the lake then disappearing again. He was tall and had dark eyes that were only shadows in this dream. Then another day came and he swam across the lake. Shogun followed the man closely in the dreams. The lake emptied into a long cave and disappeared from sight. The man liked the cave, exploring every section of its cold walls. He felt at home there, finally able to breathe in its heavy, damp air.

The tree began to notice fewer and fewer villagers coming to the lake's shore. *Peculiar.* The lake was a strange lake to start out with. Just a deep, lifeless pit with no fish. Maybe it was a dead lake, that's why it was so silent and grim. Maybe that's why the villagers avoided it for the most part. Maybe that's why there were no other trees around, it just happened to be this tree's luck that the wind stuck it there as a seedling.

Then one day, the tree noticed the man taking a villager to the cave. Under a barely lit sky, the tree was unsure if it was early morning or early night. Swimming quietly across that lifeless lake, the man would take slow and deliberate strokes, dragging the motionless body behind him. The villager would look at the tree, their eyes moving left and right. And then another day, another villager. And another. The tree started taking fewer naps, paying a bit more attention. *What was this man doing? Strange.*

And then there were no more villagers. It became very quiet to the tree, a bit eerie, actually. The man even took the wild horses that roamed those lands to the cave. This made the tree rather sad, it was so interesting to watch the horses run around and stomp in the marshy grasses. The tree would sometimes dream another dream of what it felt like to run free. Shogun asked to see more of the current dream first. The tree felt so incredibly lethargic but obliged.

One morning, the man came out of the cave angrily. It seemed like anger to the tree because his swimming strokes were rather choppy and uncoordinated, unlike the man's usual style. It had been a long time since the tree had seen the man, he looked even larger and stronger. Or the tree thought it had been a long time, it wasn't sure. Either way, the man was angry and stomped off across the grass. With each step he grew bigger and bigger, the lake water dripping from his clothes as he transformed into a monster. The tree tried to arch its branches to get a better look but lost sight of him after a while. *That was certainly strange.*

There was a break of time in the dream as the tree got distracted by a nearby bird that landed on one of its branches. The bird scuttled away when the man returned, stumbling through the grass, no longer a monster. Shogun was close behind him so the man jumped into the lake and swam as fast as he could. The tree knew it was as fast as he could because it'd never seen a pace like that before. Shogun watched himself in the dream walk around the beach and before long Madigan appeared. They talked but it sounded like a muffled murmur in the tree's dream state.

The tree didn't mind that the two people made camp near it. Actually, it was rather interesting to watch all the gadgets and such come out of the bags. The tree thought they both looked rather tired and it was making the tree tired as well. *So many yawns.* The girl fell asleep and the boy was very, very close to it, although the tree wasn't sure he meant to be. The boy fell asleep and the tree caught one last glance of the man, swimming darkly across his lake. The old tree decided it would keep watching, entertaining the boy but keeping an eye on this strange man. This was the tree's lake as well, anyway. It had a right to know what was going on.

The man circled the camp carefully. When he seemed sure that the girl and boy were asleep he approached closer and closer. Shogun could see himself moving subtly in his sleep, dreaming this dream. He tried to will himself to wake up, feeling the droplets of water touch his skin as the man walked by.

Shogun could only watch as the man went to Madigan, who was completely oblivious in the land of her deep sleep. His back was to Shogun but he could see the man wave a hand over Madigan's face and her eyes popped open, staring right at Shogun. *Good, she was awake,* Shogun thought. She'd call the wind and knock him right back to his cave. But she didn't call the wind. She didn't move a muscle. She just looked at Shogun, blinking rapidly. The man picked her up and slung her over his shoulder, stopping to look down at Shogun's sleeping body. Shogun finally saw his face, rough and old. A face truly made of shadows. He paused for a long time, what seemed rather long even to the tree. *Thinking about what to do,* the tree mused. Shogun could feel the beads of sweat gathering on his forehead and the burning heat of his axe gnawing at his back. He strained to wake up. Wake up. *Wake up!*

Then the man was gone. Shogun heard a splash and the tree told him the man was taking Madigan to the cave, like everyone else. *No sense in watching it, really. Same old, same old.* Plus, the tree felt tired. Very tired. Such a tedious dream. More time passed and it was now morning. Well, probably time for the boy to wake up anyway, hm? Yes, sounds about right. *Good night.*

Shogun jumped up with a start. The mid-morning light burned down on him where he had been slumped against the lazy tree for hours in his trapped sleep. Their camp had been scattered, whether from the man or the blustery wind or both. Madigan was gone. Her sleeping bag was still there, whipping in the wind as it slowly crawled across the beach in search of her. It hadn't been a dream, it had been real. He reached behind him and felt his axe still locked tightly to his sweaty back. The man hadn't seen it, protected between Shogun and the tree. Up in the sky, the outline of the flame was gone. Shogun felt his pulse begin to pick up. The wind pushed against him and that lazy tree was no help to him, having lulled back into its oblivious haze. He had to calm down and think. Calm down and think. Be calm and think.

"He's taken her to the place with the others," a voice called out.

Shogun whirled around. A man stood up from where he had been camouflaged in the marsh, blending in as though he was a blade of grass himself, waving endlessly in that endless wind. His skin was tan and smooth, likely from the constant light and lack of shadows at these Southern Lakes. The man's eyes were large and heavy. He stepped out and held his hands up to Shogun. A younger man stepped out from behind him as well, hands held up in a similar show of surrender. Shogun recognized their hesitant outlines. Passive opponents, too passive to do anything but watch.

"Who is he?" Shogun asked breathlessly. He felt he was still gasping to catch his breath after that exhausting dream. That dream had drained him, the tree moved at such a slow pace that it even slowed Shogun's respiration rate.

The men exchanged looks. Weary, haggard looks. Their dark hair hung into their eyes and their clothes did not appear to have been washed in a very long time. The older man spoke up. He had speckled flecks of gray throughout his hair, like stars against the dark night sky.

"He was once one of us, from our village. What name he goes by now, I do not know. He used to be called Felin. But he is not the same man I once called my brother."

"There are others?" Shogun had dreamed that there were, but he wasn't sure how much that lazy tree really grasped.

"Yes, but we are all that's left."

"What's he doing with them?" Shogun pressed.

The younger man stepped up. Shogun's axe warmed up a bit. This one was the one to the watch. This was the one who wanted to take action.

"He's trying to take their spirits. He thinks they will make him more powerful," he spoke up. He looked the strongest of the two, his muscles visible through his thin shirt. "He has our family, our children. Even our spirit brothers and sisters."

"Spirit brothers?"

He was talking about the horses, the tree yawned. These villagers believed they have spirit partners in this world, the wild horses that roam across the marshlands. Extensions of themselves, the tree supposed. Rather exhausting it seemed to the tree, running around everywhere like that. These villagers and their spirits.

"We couldn't stop him..." the older man's voice trailed off, as though the shame of it was too much to verbalize. "He's turned into something else."

Shogun looked over his shoulder at the still lake. Seemingly innocent yet something just didn't feel quite right. "I saw him wave his hand over my friend's face and she was paralyzed," Shogun turned back to them. "What is that?"

"He's always had a...way," the older man answered. "But it has manifested into something darker. I fear what power it has given him." He hung his head heavily.

"And he spared you?"

"No," the younger man spoke up. His eyes blazed. "He left us to suffer."

"You defeated his creature," the old man interrupted. "We saw it. How?"

"It wasn't me. It was the girl with me. I need to get to that cave. Now."

Both men shook their heads at the same time. "No, that is not a place you want to go. We've discussed this many times and we need to catch him while -"

"No," Shogun stopped them firmly. "We attack him where he feels safe." He began gathering and rolling up whatever supplies were left and tied them firmly to the tree. A bit too firmly, probably. He didn't trust this tree would have enough sense to keep a watchful eye out without a little help.

The men watched him, hesitantly waiting for the wind to sway them in the correct direction. But it was as silent and still as a tomb. Shogun removed his axe and stood in front of them. "What are your names?"

The old man closed his eyes. "I no longer have a name. I am not the man I was before," he replied. His face was so weary that it drooped before Shogun's very eyes.

"What *was* your name?" Shogun insisted levelly. He understood this power of the name. Ragoon had taught him that, as well. You are who you are because of your name. And your name is backed by your actions or lack of actions. By your right or wrong moves. To shame yourself is to fail your name. And that is to fail yourself.

"They called me King," he finally answered. He wept to himself heavily, miserably.

"And I am Darian," the young man answered. He lowered his voice. "Felin's son."

Now Shogun understood. He understood the hesitancy. The fear and the shame. He understood more than those men could ever know. He showed the two men his axe. It glowed in his hand, lighting their faces. Whispering words only Shogun could understand.

"This is my spirit brother," he told them. "And it will stop him, I am sure of it."

XXI

THE LOST SPIRIT BROTHER

The air was heavy with moisture. It was old moisture, it had existed there many years. It gathered on the cave walls and remained there for long amounts of time, slowly accumulating and dripping down the cave rock when the timing was right. The rock had become slick from years of water travelling down like this over and over, smoothing its once ragged surface. Then the water would finally reach the cave floor, where a footstep or slight breeze would take it outside to let the sun do as it will. And then the water would evaporate into the air until it reached the clouds, where it would be carried back to the still lake. There it would eventually return home and start the cycle all over again. This was what it wanted here in this dark, cold place.

Madigan touched the water on the cave wall carefully. There was no light in this place and no sound but her breathing. All she knew was the quiet story of that water and its quest for the sun. She followed its long journey in her mind and learned the tunnels of the cave and that she was very far away from the entrance. But it was more than she knew before, as her only memory of the previous hours were of water and movement and darkness. Then she woke up, shaking uncontrollably in the chill of the cave. For a moment she thought she was still asleep, dreaming of a dark face with no eyes.

The dust sprite came to her aide with warmth and told her this was not a dream. It warmed her without light as to not draw attention. The dust sprite had seen him long before he had reached Madigan and Shogun's camp, skulking through the water like a snake. It knew Madigan and Shogun were too still to stop him. So the dust sprite held on with all its might as the man dragged Madigan through the water. It must not leave her side. They had made a promise, her and the dust sprite.

Who is he, Madigan asked the water droplets. They told her of his passing and goings but not much else. He was a vehicle to them and that was all. And Madigan knew nothing herself. He had masked himself within his creature of water. He had taken her from sleep without waking her. He could be sitting right next to her for all she knew. And maybe he was. She asked the dust sprite to shine some light. It was a risk she was willing to take.

The dust sprite cast a low, gradual glow. Slowly, faces began to light around Madigan. Thin, gaunt faces with empty eyes staring at her without surprise, as though they had seen her in the thick darkness all along. Madigan felt her throat clench and the dust sprite stayed close to her side. They were alive but not right. Dozens of men, women, and children. Breathing and blinking, but missing something behind their eyes. Madigan opened her mouth to speak but one child shook his head. He looked behind him and pointed.

Madigan understood enough. She stood up and started running, the dust sprite following right behind her. She trusted her mind even more than the dull light from the dust sprite. Those droplets had no reason to mislead her. She would find her way out. She would find the sun and maybe take a few of the droplets with her. Run, run, running from a force Madigan couldn't see or feel. But something was coming. Her gut was telling her she was almost within its grasp. *Run fast, fast, faster.* She stumbled and then the dust sprite flashed and everything went black.

She awoke again with a chill. Soaked to her core, waking with a rush of air as though she had just broke through the surface of water after a long time beneath its depths. This place was different than the cave with the droplets. It was a deep, damp chamber with lanterns hanging from the walls, casting murky light as if she was on a ship at sea. Her eyes focused and Madigan realized she was trapped in some sort of makeshift cell, composed of piled rocks and a wire door. The cell had a purpose. And she was not the first one to be here.

The door was locked. Madigan began searching around the filthy enclosure with her hands, looking for some route of escape.

"Dust sprite!" she whispered loudly.

"There's no one else here," a deep voice spoke from across the room. Stepping into the light was the man she had seen in the place of the water creature, Madigan was sure of it. She knew his face without seeing it. She knew his presence even without feeling it.

"My name is Felin," he continued. The man had dark hair and black eyes. His skin was a strange color, tan and stretched. "Who are you?" he asked.

"Let me out of here," Madigan whispered. She tried to control her fear. It shook inside of her, trembling to come out. She couldn't let him see.

"Not yet. Soon," he replied stiffly.

"What do you want?"

Felin paused, considering his answer. "I need what makes you. I need your spirit."

"I don't understand."

"How did you break apart my creature?" Felin asked, appearing genuinely curious. He sauntered up to the cell door and stared through the thick wires, looking Madigan up and down.

Madigan didn't respond. She looked around the chamber, studying it.

"I heard you in my head," Felin insisted, leaning closer and closer to the cell door. He brushed back his damp hair and Madigan got a full view of his eyes. In them, she recognized a darkness she had seen before and her fear was replaced with fury.

"You attacked us," she replied, approaching the cell door as well. She turned to look him in the eye. "So yes, I pulled you apart, drop by drop."

Felin slammed his head against the cell door, causing Madigan to jump back. "And it will never happen again!" he screamed.

Madigan pushed up to the back of the cell as far as she could go. Felin was yelling and speaking words she could make no sense of, reaching for her through the bars. Her heart jumped up into her throat, beating and warning her to react. She felt herself being pulled towards Felin without her control. Madigan closed her eyes and called to the water droplets. She reached out to them and asked them to hurry to her. Summon their brothers and sisters from the lake. She would give them their moment in the sun, come to her quickly.

Water began to slide down the walls, seeping through the cracks in the stone. It poured off the lanterns like rainstorms of light. The sound of moving water grew louder and louder, splashing against Felin's legs and pooling under Madigan as she scratched to get away. Quietly, the droplets climbed up Felin's legs, beneath his clothes, and up his torso until finally stopping at his neck. They gathered there, contemplating. Beading thicker and thicker.

In his fury, Felin didn't notice the droplets until they began to squeeze. Until they snuck into his open mouth that was gasping for air. Madigan watched as Felin swung around the room, writhing into tables and other objects in the chamber. Now the water was rushing into the room at an alarming speed, up to Madigan's knees from where she was fumbling with the cell door. She tried to tell the water droplets to calm themselves, but they had become too excited at the thought of sun and freedom. *Sun and freedom.* They had to get there. No time to listen. Faster. Faster. Faster.

In the far distance, she heard her name. An echo of an echo like she had heard once before. "Shogun!" she screamed over and over. She could barely hear her own voice over the thundering water. But maybe he would hear her voice, echoing echoes in his own mind.

• • •

"Madigan!"

Shogun held his breath as he listened. His call echoed down the chambers of the cave with no response. He adjusted his sweaty grip on his axe and called out again. Her name traveled down the cave tunnels again but was answered only by drips of silence.

He had been exploring the cave for a long time. King and Darian had taken separate paths and occasionally Shogun could hear their own calls in the distance. His own progress felt painfully slow as he put one foot in front of the other, pushing through the wet black air with only the glow of his axe to show the way. Occasionally he would swing his axe out in front of him, imagining the man a breath ahead. He had no other sense of direction, no bearing in that suffocating darkness. He wiped the sweat from his forehead as he tried to calm the panic in his chest. If Shogun could have imagined the setting of his worst nightmare, this was it. A world without light or trees or air, hidden beneath the ground and filling with water painfully slow as it drip, drip, dripped down the impenetrable walls. He closed his eyes for one moment to escape. Then in the far distance, he heard his name.

"Madigan!" Shogun shouted again, breaking into a run to chase the sound of her voice. He kept one hand on the slimy wall to steady himself and the other on his axe, held in front of him like a torch. The pulse of the axe's glow seemed to sync with his racing heartbeat. It built and built until blurring into a fireball. Shogun stopped and looked down at his feet. Tucked against the base of the chamber wall was a small hole. He stooped down to inspect it and felt the rough edges of the hole, chipped and trimmed. It was just large enough to fit through. Shogun lowered his axe into the hole and saw the reflection of choppy water sloshing back and forth. This time, he heard his name loud and clear.

Shogun strapped his axe onto his back and dropped through the hole, almost submerged by the rising water. He began wading through the chamber, shielding his eyes from the swinging, flashing lanterns.

"Where are you?" he called out, pushing through the debris.

"Here!" Madigan shouted as loud as she could, waving through the bars.

"What in the..." Shogun cursed, pulling at the bars. "What is this? Where is he?"

Madigan pointed to Felin's floating body. "He's dead. Just get me out of here!"

Shogun motioned for Madigan to stand back. He lifted his axe off his back and tried to steady himself in the waist deep water. The axe glowed hot to everything but Shogun's touch. He stared at the bars hard and with one swing his axe sliced through cleanly. In an instant, he had swung back the other direction, cutting another layer of bars off with it. Madigan crawled through the small opening, never so glad to see that ugly axe.

The water had become so excited by the commotion that now it rushed at an even faster speed. It was going to see the sun and that was nothing to slow down for. Shogun and Madigan swam back towards the entrance of the chamber, unable to speak above the rushing water. Then Shogun was gone. Madigan fought to stay above water and looked around. Felin was gone, too.

The two men broke through the water's surface, Shogun's arm hooked around Felin's neck. They thrashed above and below the rising water, Madigan only able to keep track of them by Shogun's glowing axe. She closed her eyes and plead with the water droplets to give him room. Give Shogun room to finish this for good and then they would truly be free. Let him stop the man that kept them in darkness.

The water droplets parted. Just for a bit. Curious as to what this man could do. *A good man,* she had said. Curious enough that they would halt their trek and watch. Sliding to the sides of the chamber and up the ceiling, the water droplets climbed away, leaving Shogun and Felin on the glistening dry ground. Shogun stood over Felin and lifted his axe high behind him. Madigan closed her eyes but still saw a stream of light and then the sound of the axe hitting the hard rock ground. The water exhaled and came crashing back as lines of black blood floated to the surface of the water, gathering in clumps of sticky foam. Shogun appeared above the surface again and replaced the axe to his back, spitting into the black foam.

Now water was pouring through the small hole that provided the only entrance and exit to the chamber. More water droplets had heard of the fight and wanted to come and watch. There were too many for Madigan to reason with now. A thousand voices all excitably talking at once. The last of the lanterns became engulfed in water and Madigan and Shogun were left in complete darkness, treading water and grasping for each other. Was this her end, Madigan wondered. Lost in the dark, doomed by her brothers and sisters. Left to float endlessly in that chamber for ages and ages.

A light glowed beneath the water, weaving in and out between the underwater obstacles. The dust sprite burst above the water and Madigan's hair stood on end in recognition of its light. The dust sprite circled around her happily, bouncing around what was left of the room. It pulsed and rolled over to the exit hole, bobbing in and out. Without a word, Shogun and Madigan swam over to the hole and climbed through, struggling against the strong current of the water. Once through, they fell to the cave floor breathlessly, coughing up swallowed water and trying to get their bearings in the small circle of light provided by the dust sprite.

Shogun stood up and made sure his axe was still on his back. He inhaled a huge gulp of air and helped Madigan up. She was shaking from the inside out, unable to process anything in that pit. There was something about this place that drained her, every part of her. Taking a little bit at a time, hoping to be inconspicuous. But she noticed. A little pinprick every time. She looked at Shogun. She would have died if not for him. A little bit at a time.

"Thank you," she whispered, reaching for Shogun. She held him in a tight embrace, her arms completely wrapped around his torso. His clothes were soaked but she felt the warmth of his body and it connected somewhere deep within her. He had called to her and she had called to him. Their minds had searched and found one another even in the darkness. Slowly, Shogun wrapped his arms around her and he could feel her shaking body calm with each deliberate breath. This touch was nothing he had felt before. A connection made from one body to the other, his heart beating against her heart. Faster and faster. It stirred in him a feeling he could not describe. And he didn't want to let it go.

A light approached in the distance, wavering and flickering in the dampness. A man's voice called out, echoing off the cave walls. It was Darian. The dust sprite retreated to Madigan's hair quickly, afraid to complicate things more by its presence. Although it had been curious to observe what was developing.

"Follow me!" Darian shouted, waving his arms, an outline against the torchlight. Madigan and Shogun let go of each other and followed the light, through the endless cave, until they saw the freedom of outdoors. The water droplets had been right, if only Madigan had been given the chance.

The evening light glowed amber as giant clouds filled the hazy sky. On the small beach outside the cave were dozens of people, pale even in that soft light. The faces of the same people that Madigan had seen in the dark cave, blank and emotionless. Now they cried and hugged one another, only stopping to cheer quietly when Shogun and Madigan finally emerged.

Madigan blinked at the harshness of the soft twilight after so many hours of darkness. She looked to the sky. The flame was gone, no outline or hint of it remained. She knew it was gone even before looking. Had it given up when she left, unable to sense her through the thick cave walls? Maybe it had simply moved on without them, relentlessly charging forward, no time to look back for Shogun or herself.

Darian's eyes welled with tears. He clapped Shogun on the shoulder, discarding the torch now that they were safely outdoors.

"My family is alive," he choked, pointing to a woman and child not far from him. "We owe you everything."

"I know he was your father…" Shogun's voice trailed off. He felt the dull remaining heat from his axe against his back, still stained with blood.

"No," Darian shook his head. "That man was gone a long time ago." He looked to Madigan. "You," he added. "You are the one he went after. You are the one who destroyed the monster."

"We both did," Madigan replied, looking over at Shogun.

"How can we repay you?"

"I believe I know how," another voice answered. It was King, standing a bit taller, soaking wet like the others. "I believe I know what you are looking for."

XXII

THE LOST WANDERER RETURNS

He told the story of a day not so long ago, the day when he first noticed that glint of darkness in his dear wife's eyes. It was a warm, late summer evening. She had been outside working on the garden, the softly setting sun highlighting the golden strands in her hair. He held their tiny son in his arms and watched from the kitchen window, admiring her quietly. Thinking how lucky he was that she belonged to him and that he belonged to her. A wind stirred her and she gazed far into the distance, over the hills and treetops. When she turned to look at the man, her unfamiliar gaze startled him. It must've been the light. It must've been the impending night, he told himself. Because those dark eyes did not belong to his beloved wife.

That night, sitting in his evening chair with his drink, he watched his wife rock their child to sleep. Their small baby was wrapped safely in his crib, falling softly into his dreams. She rocked the cradle rhythmically, her shadow dancing in the nearby firelight. She whispered to herself and stared just past the edge of the cradle. Rocking back and forth. Back and forth. She looked up at her husband and froze his blood with her cold stare. He took a long drink. The wind howled outside their little house on the little hill, rattling the windows. He would forever remember its calls. And how he should have listened.

When he woke the next morning, he was startled to find himself still in his chair, drink by his side. The sun was on his face, slowly inching forward hour by hour until it finally reached him, urging him to wake up. The front door was swinging open, allowing the cold morning air to whisk into the house. He remembered it smelled like autumn, damp and aromatic. Across the room, his son's cradle rocked gently. He stumbled over to find it empty, only tended by the sad wind. Rocking it back and forth. Back and forth. He called out and wept from the deepest depths of his soul. He would find them hours later, on the bank of the nearby river. Long, long gone. Days turned into nights. Then he finally dreamt the dream that sent him in search for his family. He saw them, imprisoned in what appeared to be a tower, hidden away in a faraway place. Whatever it was, he saw himself there, clear as day. And he dreamt that his wife was back at his side, carrying their son, her eyes bright and shining once again.

Shogun and Madigan listened to the story in silence, sitting in the warm light of King's home. It was a small, cluttered house in the heart of the little village that was slowly stirring back to life. His home smelled of strong spices and smoke, burning their nostrils. King told his story, raising his voice and closing his eyes with the ups and downs of the tale. When he was finished, he stood up and paced the floor.

"I was told that story by my grandfather. He met a man that told him this tale by this very fireside," King whispered, staring at the fire. He turned to Shogun and Madigan. "But I believe it has something to do with you. I knew it the first time I saw you in the darkness."

Shogun met his gaze. He was dressed in dry clothes and drinking a large glass of warm liquid poured for him by King. It burned his throat but King had told him it would chase away any remaining bad spirits that had attached to him. The hair on his neck had been standing on edge during the story. He was transported back in time to his own grandfather's colorful storytelling. *A search for a faraway place that would save his family.* Shogun's mind raced as he searched back through his memories.

Madigan listened intently. She was wrapped in several blankets, sitting as close to the fire as she could. The chill from the cave was slowly leaving her, flicker by flicker. The flames could sense the dampness inside of her and raged to fight extinguishment. The dust sprite was sleeping soundly in the layers of her finally dry hair. Dreaming of soft, wavy places.

"You saw Felin's eyes?" King asked, looking from Shogun to Madigan. "They are a sign of what's to come. Again."

Madigan looked over at Shogun. She saw his thoughts written across his face. "What happened to the man?" she asked finally.

King considered his response for a long time. A log fell over in the silence, sending flames licking into the air and causing thoughts to rise from the ashes.

"They say," King replied slowly. "He is still alive."

"They say," Madigan repeated slowly. She had grown skeptical of anyone from the Southern Lakes. The dust sprite was beginning to stir, opening one eye to keep informed.

Shogun finished the last of his drink with one large gulp. "Where is he?" he asked, avoiding Madigan's gaze.

"If what I hear is true, then he lives in the Snowy North Mountain."

"How do we get there?" Shogun pressed.

"You can take a train north, through the Central Forest," King advised. He paused and studied Shogun and Madigan's faces, looking very young in that soft firelight. "Was I right to tell you this? Do you know what is happening, what took my brother from me?"

"I don't know," Shogun replied. "But I will find out."

King bowed his head. "Then I will do all I can to help you. I promise you that."

"We will leave in the morning," Shogun said to Madigan. He would have left that moment if not for her exhausted slump. She was due her quiet sleep, her few hours of peaceful rest.

Madigan nodded slowly. Her flame was gone and she had no sense of what direction it took off in. Not even a lingering thought. She felt abandoned but maybe the flame had its reasons. At this point, it was the thought of leaving the Southern Lakes that prompted her answer more than anything. "Agreed."

The next morning, the sky was a pale gray, different than their other mornings at the Southern Lakes. Shogun found it to be a familiar glimpse of home. He stood outside and focused his mind. He had risen before anyone else so he could capture this silence for himself. He thought back to a day, to a dark house with a man no longer a man. Shogun could sense his axe burning for him beside his bed, remembering the same moment and that cut of flesh. His own father. He repeated the words over again in his mind. *He had killed his own father.* And maybe he didn't have to.

Shogun glanced over as Madigan joined him outside, wrapped in layers of blankets. Her hair stretched in a dozen different directions from hours of sleep, her eyes heavy but rested. She stood next to him, almost shoulder to shoulder.

"It's very early," she murmured, stretching as she yawned.

Shogun didn't answer.

"Stop thinking of that," Madigan said, looking down at her bare feet. When he looked at her, she shrugged her shoulders. "The dust sprite may have told me a thing or two."

Shogun smirked sourly. "I keep getting tempted back."

"There was nothing left of him," Madigan insisted.

Shogun searched the sky. He breathed deeply. "King's story last night," he whispered, turning to Madigan. "Did it remind you of another?"

Madigan nodded. "Old Roland's story. The man and the compass."

"Maybe it wasn't a story after all," Shogun continued. "And the dust sprites. What they told us. If it's all connected..."

"What does that mean for us?"

"I don't know."

Madigan watched the quietly rising sun. It was almost complete sunrise, the time to gather and leave. Brushstrokes painted across the gray sky, wisps of light emerging one layer at a time. She could feel Shogun's thoughts as he began to wander into the depths of doubt, peering into a dark hole he may not be able to climb out of. She was not used to him wavering.

"I believe that you did what was right that day," she said. "And every day after, for that matter."

Shogun looked down at her. Madigan was unveiled, her guard and careful words dissolved in that moment between night and day. He paused for a long time, remembering.

"I did save you," he said, looking back at the sunrise. "That's all that matters."

· · ·

It was a several hour ride to the train station. King took Shogun and Madigan with the last few horses remaining, thin and frail creatures anxious to run free. Felin had not broken them and they would keep running to prove it. They could see the train coming towards them from very far way, steaming over the flat landscape. Beginning as a dot and inching closer, hotly charging across the ancient railway, calling out a whistle like the shrill song of the long grasses.

The train halted to a screeching stop at the remote station, which consisted of a clearing in the grass with a few boards to keep the feet dry. The train was spitting steam and dripping with heat, stained an orange tarnish from years of wear and rare up-keep. The smell of hot fuel singed their noses and eyes. The conductor stepped from the engine, a tall man covered with soot and sweat, wearing clothes that may have been white at one time but were now an indistinguishable and muddled gray. His bright eyes beamed through layers of wrinkles and dirt.

"King," the conductor greeted simply. "Been awhile."

"Yes," King replied. He stood on the platform and shook the conductor's hand. When they released, it was black with soot.

The conductor turned to Shogun and Madigan and studied them hard. Looking them up and down, evaluating and coming to conclusions with just that one glance. He jerked his head towards the two strangers. "Who's this?"

"This is Shogun and Madigan. They need to get to the Snowy North Mountain. I told them you could get them there."

The conductor raised a bushy eyebrow. "What're you after?" he asked them.

"I told them of…the old man in the mountain," King replied.

Madigan watched their exchange closely. The conductor met King's gaze and lingered there. He took a deep breath and adjusted his hat.

"Hm. Got to go through the forest first, you know."

"Yes, sir. We know," Shogun replied, stepping forward. "We still need to get north. What will it cost?"

The conductor waved his hand. It took him awhile to follow it up, as though he initially thought the hand wave said it all. "No need for payment. Going north, anyway. There's a settlement at the base of the mountains, I'm taking some supplies that way."

"Thank you, Rufus," King said, bowing his head.

"She's coming, too?" Rufus asked, jerking his hand towards Madigan. He made quick eye contact with her but looked away.

"Yes, she's coming, too," Madigan replied dryly.

"Hm," Rufus added. He spat a large wad of black tar out of his mouth to the ground, where it appeared to sizzle against the ground. The grass wilted beneath its suffocating pitch. "Alright, let's go."

XXIII

THE CENTRAL FOREST

Shogun could breathe again. Shallow breaths at first, as though he was learning respiration again. His mind felt dry from the lengthy silence he had endured, a drought of thoughts leaving his mind parched and cracked. But now he was alive again. He could smell the trees from a mile away, feel the whispers of the wind through the branches and taste the musky undergrowth. He welcomed the damp chill that made home in his bones, making him stronger for it. He knew the hidden corners of the furthest shadows as though he had designed them himself, constructing them out of his own imagination. His heart leapt in recognition of the familiar flicker of flashing sunlight that raced alongside the train, jumping out at any break in the tree line. Blinding yet revealing, almost surreal if not for the proof of its warmth on the palm of his hand. He closed his eyes and listened silently to the approaching voices. The trees saw him coming. Their Shogun. Their little boy. *Our hopes and dreams, home again.*

He was standing on the platform outside the train car, breathing in every breath he could get. The air was forceful and free, pressing him in the face at breakneck speed, almost to the point where he couldn't keep up with it. He was so overwhelmed with air there was no time for oxygen. Shogun imagined his blood pulsing evergreen and a million lights going off in his mind. He was whole again, reconstructed from a collection of broken pieces. They knew each and every vein in his body. Each heartbeat was their heartbeat, pound, pound, pounding beneath the soil. He only needed to ask and they would tell him. He only needed to reach out and they would be there.

The trees reached into his mind and learned all the things he saw and did at the Southern Lakes. They watched him almost drown but rise and fight again. They saw the foolish old tree keep Shogun in a frozen sleep. They felt the adrenaline as he searched deeper and deeper into Felin's cave, his palm sweaty around the hilt of his axe, ready to swing.

Then they saw Shogun begin to light from the inside. A light that started as a tiny glow then sparked into a flame. Caused by a touch between him and Madigan, that girl of the sea. A feeling he was new to, unrecognizable yet instinctive. An embrace that sent that flame into a wildfire, burning hot and igniting every sense in his body. Sending smoke upwards to his mind, inducing a high that dulled all other thoughts but Madigan and that touch. The trees wondered if this was dangerous, between he and she. Because in that light they created, he only saw Madigan. Not the dangers all around him. Just he and her. Just them.

Their brothers and sisters from far away had not told them about this scenario, the trees commiserated. They had not alerted them of the impact of this tiny girl, curled asleep in a nearby bunk, dreaming of an open sea. Her dust sprite laying quietly beside her, listening to them. The trees realized what had happened in those Southern Lakes had caused Shogun to add another branch to his already intricate tree. He was reaching out to them for guidance, but they couldn't help him with this answer.

Shogun remained outside until nighttime. Until his fingers and nose were so numb that he could no longer smell the damp undergrowth and how it tasted in his mouth. He waited to see the stars and how they would appear in this night sky. How the outline of the trees would play out in that place and his state of mind. He took one last breath and turned to go inside, to sleep and dream his own dreams. The trees began to drift themselves, blissful that their Shogun was back within their arms again.

Wait, Shogun. The trees stopped him. Shogun paused with his hand on the train car door handle. His axe went from calm and collected to searing with heat, burning him through the layers on his back as though it was paper thin. Within a moment, his axe was in his hand, ready to strike the darkness. He tried to listen above the loud noises of the train but there was nothing.

Listen closer, Shogun. He heard the distant sound of hooves, thundering behind the train with a vengeance. True vengeance, the kind that would draw power from the darkness of that night. Shogun could feel the approaching presence and immediately understood the tree's averted glances. It was Ragoon. Back to hunt him. Back to haunt him.

"Rufus!" Shogun shouted, bursting into the engine room. He tried to steady himself as the rushing train went around a huge corner. Rufus was at the helm with cotton balls stuffed in his ears. He appeared to be drinking a giant mug of coffee as he sang a tune to himself.

"Hey!" Shogun shouted again, yanking Rufus' arm.

Rufus sputtered with surprise. He pulled a giant string of cotton out of one of his ears. "What's the problem, boy? You shouldn't be up here! Get on back!"

"We're going to be attacked!" Shogun shouted. "Can you speed this up?"

"Attacked? What are you talking about? Ain't nobody out here."

"Just get this train moving faster!"

Rufus shrugged. He replaced the cotton back into his ear and nodded while he took another long swig of coffee. "I suppose so," he mouthed. He began singing to himself again.

In the back of his mind, Shogun could hear the hooves pounding faster and faster. They were getting closer and they wouldn't tire, not for a second. It was the night, spurring them on into the darkness to fight, fight, fight. He knew their way of thinking. He knew the mindset they were in right now. He knew he was their prey. Eyes red with fire, they may as well be demons, specters dreamed up in the thick black where the eyes cannot penetrate. A force unable to reason with or avoid, his only chance was to fight back. Their only chance.

· · ·

She was dreaming of home. Floating on a calm, still sea. Just herself on her father's boat, the oars gone, floating peacefully yet aimlessly. She was staring hard across the water through the parting mist, squinting to see. A figure began to emerge from the fog. A tall figure, just a barely visible outline. Slowly, it came closer and closer. She was almost able to see the face when she heard a loud whistle in the distance. Quiet at first, then louder and louder until she had to cover her ears. The sea began to rumble and her boat began to rock and threatened to capsize. It was a train whistle, calling out for Madigan. She looked back one last time at the figure who had frozen, stuck in the misty haze, waiting for her to see.

A light flashed brightly before her eyes and Madigan woke up. The dust sprite was floating right in front of her face, glowing hot and intense. Once it realized she was finally awake, it began to roll around the dark room anxiously. She heard the train whistle again, long and forlorn. Her bunk was rocking wildly with the increased speed of the train. She climbed out and pulled her boots and sweater back on, struggling to stay on her feet with the twists and turns encountered on the tracks.

It was night and she was disoriented. Madigan struggled to remember her bearings as she stepped out into the dark corridor that ran along the length of the bunks. These trees, always making the night so much more thick and intense than it really needed to be. It made her feel like she was choking, like there was no air when really there was probably more than she was used to.

Then she saw a sliver of light on the floor. Silver and white, beautifully glowing softly. It triggered a stir in her heart, leaping at the idea of who it might be. Madigan looked out the window and craned her neck until she could see through the rushing tree tops. A white face stared back down at her, blinking her long lashes and smiling demurely. The moon. All this way from home, she had found her. She had followed Madigan all along, slow and steady, forced to move with the pace of the rising and falling tides. But she was here now and just in time. Madigan looked down into the face of a man on horseback, keeping pace with the train. When he realized he had caught Madigan's eye, he shouted and pointed a sword at her face.

Madigan gasped and jumped back, the dust sprite whizzing through the air erratically. There were several thuds and shouts. *Men jumping on the train,* the moon advised. *Best to get out while the getting is good,* she continued, then disappeared to check her makeup.

Stumbling down the corridor, Madigan made her way towards the engine room. Running was near impossible but the dust sprite did its best to light her way. Madigan knew she was going to have several train cars to go but maybe she had time. Maybe. She managed to open the exterior door and peeked outside. Complete, utter darkness. The moon must be flat ironing her hair now. Madigan chanced it and ran over to the next train car, yanking the door open.

"There!" a man's voice shouted from above. As Madigan shut the train car door, she caught sight of several men above her. Just their outlines, barely lit by the distant stars behind them.

This train car was ridiculously cluttered, filled with buckets of bolts and screws, cans upon cans of food, piles of rags and an old, broken radio. The dust sprite led her to a closet hidden behind a coat stand of bulky jackets. Voices escalated outside. Madigan darted into the closet and closed the door quietly as the dust sprite dulled to the faintest light, hiding behind Madigan's back for good measure.

She quieted her breath to barely breathing. She would have closed her eyes if not for trying to avoid any movement. The men entered the train car, bursting through the door loudly and knocking around the miscellaneous clutter. Slowly, the moon emerged again. Like a spotlight, her beam flickered across Madigan's face as she burst through the tree line. The beam became stronger and stronger, reading her sister's expression and knowing what she had to do. The dust sprite began to vibrate behind Madigan's back, a beating, racing little heart in the darkness.

A break in the tree line allowed for the moon to shine in all her glory and she basked in every single second of it. Looking over her shoulder, she pierced through the darkness with her icy gaze. It left her victim in a state of momentary blindness, lost in her world of bright white. A desolate place where she would appear on the horizon, a bold and strange shape. And she would come to embrace her victim, draining every drop of life from them if they looked too long.

The dust sprite shot past Madigan first, knocking down one of the men in his blinded stupor. Madigan called for the wind through the open train car door, wind that was growing colder and colder as they continued trekking further and further north. Without hesitation, it burst in with a huge blast, already empowered by the racing train speed. As though it had been waiting at the door, pacing and pumping with adrenaline, ready for the flick of Madigan's wrist. And because it had spent so much time outside, this wind was sharp to the touch, frozen at its edges and slicing across the men like knives. They screamed and fell to the ground.

The moon urged Madigan on. Whispering into her ear, powerful and crazy ideas. Violence that Madigan had never dreamed of before. *Protect yourself by any means necessary*, she whispered. That was the way of the night. Survive or die trying. The men hit by the icy wind laid stiff on the floor, their blood draining out in a dozen rivers that traveled to the open train car door, where it would drip, drip, drip all the way to the sea. The sea would taste the blood and see the past, back to their Madigan standing there, the moonlight flickering on her face. Another man rushed into the train car, recoiling momentarily as he stumbled upon his fallen comrades. He raised a sword towards Madigan.

"Where's Shogun?" he shouted above the racing railway sounds. "You need to take me to Shogun!"

Madigan waved her hand and the wind burst through another window, sending shards of glass into the man. She had seen the wind out of the corner of her eye, hovering outside the window. Heaving and shaking its head impatiently, breathing hot breath against the glass. Ready to snap.

The man groaned from the floor that was now cluttered with shards of glass, struggling to stand up. He had managed to deflect most of the glass from his face but was still reeling from the impact of the wind. Suddenly, there were several loud thuds and shouts from the roof of the car. The train hit a sharp turn and a man went flying off the side, disappearing into the snow flurries. The snowflakes were illuminated by the moon, who was fascinated by those floating white diamonds that fell from the sky. She reached her arms out and clothed herself in that heavenly softness, fashioning herself a long cape of snow. The trees were getting thicker now so she whisked her cape and disappeared, leaving Madigan in complete darkness. *Until another day, sister.*

A loud ring called out through the crisp air, ending in a long, drawn out scratching across the top of the train car. So loud it vibrated and rattled the teeth and caused even the dust sprite to wince and cover its ears. The man jumped to his feet and reached through the now open window, swinging himself outside. He gave Madigan one last look before he climbed up and out of sight.

XXIV

THE BROTHER'S OATH

The train rocked back and forth, unstable at that speed on the thin strips of railroad track. Shogun grit his teeth so hard he thought he would crack them one by one. His arms ached and then lost all feeling as he surrendered to his axe. He had to admit to himself that he no longer had the strength. It was up to his axe now, warm in his hands and stuck to his palms like hot glue. He kept pushing harder and harder against his opponent's sword until Shogun knocked him down to the roof of the train car. The man went rolling and screamed as he fell off the side of the train, into the night that swallowed him whole.

The cold night was brutal. It kept growing colder and colder, hungrier and hungrier. Shogun had seen the hot breath of the horses first, charging down the tracks after them. He saw their faces emerge one by one, brothers from his past now hunting him like prey. He wondered what ran through their minds when they saw him, standing at the back of the train, his axe calling them like a beacon. Shogun met them there, one by one. Working his way up across the cars, one by one. Ragoon had swarmed them, just as he anticipated.

Shogun was about to descend into the train car when a figure caught his eye, climbing over the edge of the train. A silhouette he recognized, even under the layers of heavy coat. He held out his hand in the darkness.

"Booker?" Shogun called out, his voice almost failing him.

"Yes! Shogun!" the man called back. He stumbled and almost fell off the train, grasping for footing. The snow was becoming thicker now, falling in little dense clouds instead of wispy ice stars. "Listen to me!"

Shogun shook his head. "No, leave!"

Booker studied Shogun carefully. Sizing him up, a different man than the one he knew before. Different yet the same. "You know we've come for you! Surrender, please!"

And Shogun did know. He knew the oath that Booker was bound to. The oath that Shogun broke when he struck Neal down cold. Shogun looked at his axe that burned hot in his hand. He didn't need to look up to know the expression in Booker's eyes had changed. His stomach turned at what he had to do. But it must be done, the trees whispered to him. *It must be done.*

Shogun returned his axe to his back. He winced at its searing heat, angry with him for disappointing it. It wasn't time to stop. It wasn't time to rest. It was time to fight. *Fight.* Shogun held up his hands to Booker and shook his head. "I won't fight you! But I'm not going with you, either!"

Booker grabbed Shogun's arm as he staggered past him. Their eyes met, gazes different than when they were friends of Ragoon. Once comrades in arms, now enemies on the edge. Literally one sudden movement away from darkness, capable of sending the other into the black abyss of the forest. Shogun yanked his arm free and continued over the side of the train, climbing in through the broken window.

Madigan and the dust sprite were standing in the corner of the train car, listening to the bustle on top of the train. If Shogun had not sensed she was there he would have missed her, camouflaged in the layers of coats and rags and old blankets. The wind was casually blowing through the room, drawing the eye and ready to strike at Madigan's very blink.

Without a word, Madigan brought Shogun a blanket, filthy but dry. The dust sprite twirled around him with warm light. It was then he realized he was soaked with snow, his muscles stiffening and joints locking as the cold slowly tried to turn him into one of their own. Just a few more moments now, maybe it could reach his heart. There it would blow an icy kiss, startling the beating muscle to lose momentum and succumb to its quiet sleep. Eternal sleep, if it got the chance.

Madigan brushed Shogun's frosty hair out of his face. She touched his face and it burned hot. She had listened to his footsteps on the roof of the train, counting his breaths along with her own. Wishing the trees to help him. To bring him back, to keep him from the darkness that was spinning by them. She had never really reached out to the trees, but these trees didn't know her. Maybe they would be curious. So she had closed her eyes and wished.

"We need to get to the engine room. They'll try to stop the train so the others can catch up," Shogun panted, his heart pumping again. The ice had no chance now. It began to melt off Shogun in defeat.

"Who are they? What do they want?" Madigan asked. The dust sprite was perched on her shoulder. Watching and listening.

"It's Ragoon. I killed one of their men. And now they're out for me."

They were thrown to the ground as the train screeched to a stop. A chilling scream of metal on metal rang out in the silent forest. Sparks lit up outside the train and sizzled to an end in the snow. Shouts came from several cars down. Shogun tried to listen to the trees. He could barely hear them above the blood rushing through his ears. They were a thousand voices, swirling and talking over each other, one voice slowly filtering out at a time.

"Damn! Too late," Shogun cursed, struggling to his feet.

"Rufus…" Madigan whispered. "If we lose him…"

"We won't lose him," Shogun said, dropping the blanket to the ground and charging out into the night. Madigan took one last look out the window. If the moon had any intention of coming back, this was the time.

When they reached the engine room, Shogun and Madigan found Rufus backed into the corner, his sooty hands held up at sword point. The engine room was hot and sweaty, a strange pocket of heat in that world of cold white. The man holding the sword turned and looked at them as they entered. It was Jel, Shogun's master from Ragoon. The tiny man smirked as he looked at Shogun and nodded in recognition.

"You never came back, recruit," Jel stated, his face painfully red beneath his thick red hair. "And that's only the beginning."

"I don't suppose you've come all this way to hear my side of the story?" Shogun asked sourly.

"You've created a big problem for yourself, son."

"Did you know what Neal was about to do?" Shogun asked, his voice building. "That he was killing innocents?" *He knew*, his axe told him. *He knew.*

"You killed one of your brothers! That supersedes all else!" Jel's voice boomed, turning the sword in Shogun's direction. He shoved Rufus to the side and motioned for his old student. "And you know what I am bound to do."

Shogun straightened as he removed his axe from his back. He hoped the pain was not too visible on his numb face. He felt as though his arms were draped in weights. Like the muscles in his legs had stiffened with age. The only thing that remained light and effortless was his blade. The axe snapped to attention once Jel's eyes laid upon it.

"Found yourself an enchanted weapon, have you?" Jel laughed. His own weapon was bordering the length of his body, both thick and stocky. "It still won't help."

Madigan put her hand on Shogun's damp shoulder. The dust sprite was loudly urging her to stop him. He wouldn't win this fight. *Not this time.*

"Don't," she whispered, keeping her eyes on Jel. "You can't do this."

"I have to. We need to get north," Shogun whispered back. He looked her straight in the eye. "No matter what, get us north."

Jel lunged forward and tried to knock the axe out of Shogun's hand. It remained in Shogun's grasp and burned bright red, matching the hue of Jel's face as he became lost in the blade's reflection. The clashing metal of their weapons rang out as they thrashed around the engine room, their heavy breaths loud like shouts in the still air. Shogun felt his dwindling strength draining from him at an alarming speed. He had never felt such fatigue. Each blow felt a hundred times more magnified than the one before. He felt the air leave his lungs, burning for oxygen. Shogun slumped to the ground, darkness washing over him. If he could have slept for a thousand years, he would have. He heard a loud ringing in his ears mixed with Madigan's screams. Footsteps swirled around him and everything went black.

Booker held back one of Jel's strikes to Shogun's limp body that was crumpled on the floor of the engine room. The Ragoon master looked down with eyes wide as his blade pushed against Booker's. He let go and backed up breathlessly. Madigan and Rufus rushed over to Shogun's side as Jel and Booker circled each other.

"You…out, now!" Jel ordered, pointing at the door with his sword.

Booker shook his head. He cursed under his breath, his leather gloves creaking as he tightened his grip on his own sword.

"I can't," Booker answered, a slight waver in his voice. "Shogun is one of my brothers."

Jel laughed, raising his sword again. "Unbelievable!"

"Believe it," Madigan whispered, looking at Jel from the corner of her eye. She was staring out the window, her hand over Shogun's head that laid unconscious in her lap. A form was lurking outside the window, leaving crystals of ice as it tapped its fingertips across the glass. Its shoulders bristled and grew higher and higher, forcing it to hunch down to see through the foggy window. Looking for Madigan's signal.

Both men looked to her as the engine room began to rattle. Lines splintered through the icy glass like cracks in a frozen lake. In a heartbeat, the wind inhaled Jel through the window, his short body sucked into the sky and out of sight. *Do as you will*, Madigan told the wind, closing her eyes. *The moon will meet you on the horizon.*

Booker let out a heavy sigh and looked around the room. "Who did that? What did that?" he asked.

"It was her," Rufus said quietly, standing up and moving away from Madigan.

"Get the train going again. Please, quickly," Madigan ordered, wiping the blood from Shogun's forehead. The dust sprite inspected his wounds but determined he would be fine.

As Rufus began preparations, Booker knelt down beside them on the floor. He studied Shogun's face as Madigan watched him carefully.

"Why?" she asked.

"He helped me a time or two," Booker answered, remembering. He paused and smirked. "Actually, more than that." He stood up and returned his sword to his sheath. The train began to steam and slowly roll to a start. "I have to go."

"You can stay with us. I'll tell him —"

"No," Booker said, stepping to the engine room door. He whistled into the darkness and a horse appeared from the woods, anxiously pacing on the edges of the railroad tracks. "I'll meet up with

the others, tell them Jel took Shogun. That'll buy you some time."
He looked over his shoulder before he disappeared into the dark
white. "Tell him good luck."

With a jerk, the train gained momentum, building back towards its previous speed. Madigan sat up against the wall of the
engine room, tucking herself around Shogun to keep them both
warm. It was his turn to sleep a peaceful sleep. Rufus watched
her and the dust sprite from the helm, silent as he continued
their trek north towards the mountain in the distance. A mountain no one could see but only sense, growing larger and larger
with each turn. Watching the train and waiting.

XXV

THE SNOWY NORTH MOUNTAIN

The ridges and mountains on his head intrigued her. He was motionless in the early morning light, besides the steady heaving of his chest as he breathed in and out. She ran her fingers through the forests of his mind, listening to their whispers and shouts. The voices calling out to him in his dreams, all fighting for their chance to get to him. A moment of his time, free from outside distractions that needed his attention. Where they could unveil and unwrap all the thoughts he had locked away behind a thousand doors, to a place even he didn't know existed.

Morning burned bright, revealing the starkness of the snow outside. They had completely left behind the rain-drenched branches and were now in a world purely made of crystal white. There were miles and miles of ice palaces and trees locked in place by the heavy frozen water. Sleeping peacefully, dreaming heavy dreams just like Shogun. A mischievous wind would bluster by and shake the ice and snow away, waking the tree from its limbo. Blinking in the light, the tree would gather its wits and realize it was only winter. It would soak in the beauty until the snow sent it to sleep again, whispering a quiet lullaby as it drifted through the sky, covering the tree again in a soft blanket, cold and safe. Go to sleep. *Sleep, sleep, sleep forever.*

The train had run relentlessly through the night. Madigan had stayed awake through it all, afraid to drift into the stillness of sleep. Rufus navigated the train but watched them, stealing occasional curious glances at the dust sprite that slept on Madigan's shoulder. She would meet his gaze and she didn't like it. And if the dust sprite had been awake, it would think that, too. She grew aware of his observing looks that he always followed up with a smile and a nod. She glared back at him. *Nothing strange to see here. Just move along.*

The cold wind woke Shogun, burning his warm cheeks with its crisp touch. He sat up slowly, lethargic from the heavy sleep that had kept him captive for hours. Madigan watched as his mind awakened and remembered. He looked over at her, questioning.

"It was Booker," Madigan told him. "And he said good luck."

Shogun hung his head. "He's the one that will need the luck." He wanted to envision his friend riding through the forest, the sun breaking through the trees as he raced in the opposite direction of Ragoon. He wanted to believe that was what happened but knew otherwise.

"There she is," Rufus announced, glancing over his shoulder. "The Snowy North Mountain herself."

Shogun jumped up to look out the broken engine room window, Madigan stiffly joining him by his side. The Snowy North Mountain was a looming giant, piercing through the air magnificently. Staring them down, aiming right for the gut, reaching for them across the expanse. Whatever Shogun had imagined in his mind was far from this.

A mixture of many things pumped through their veins, whether it was fear or excitement or dread or relief or the mountain itself. A hot concoction boiled in Shogun's stomach. Never before had he seen a mountain like that. Spindly, large dark trees grew on its tallest heights, ageless sentinels growing higher and higher into the sky. He felt the mountain take his breath and hold it in its firm grasp, right in front of his face.

To say, *look, I hold your life in my hand. To take or leave as I wish.*

Madigan eyed the mountain, exchanging cautious glances with the dust sprite. That mountain was too large and full of too many hidden corners. Her mind wandered, reached, to what could lay in those corners and a chill shot up her back. She knew Shogun's heart was racing beside her. That mountain was calling to him, luring him with its siren song, promising him great heights and even greater answers. *Call all you wish,* Madigan thought. You can reach Shogun, but never her. She averted her eyes when the mountain locked in on her. You can reach Shogun, but never her.

The train approached the settlement at the base of the Snowy North Mountain. It steamed past decrepit buildings and overgrown mills. There were no lights or signs of life, as though the town was frozen in time. The train halted to a stop in the empty station that was covered by a thick layer of ice.

"I thought he said he was bringing supplies. This town is abandoned," Madigan whispered to Shogun as she buttoned up the heavy jacket Rufus had provided her. She coughed at its stench, a mixture of smoke and mold. The dust sprite took a deep breath before diving in.

Shogun nodded, struggling with his own heavy jacket. It was made of thick, coarse furs from animals he was not familiar with. "I know. Just be wary."

Rufus watched them from the other end of the engine room, where he was strapping a large bag of supplies to his back. He smirked at their hushed conversation.

"All ready, now?" he called to them, tossing a pack to each of them.

"Where are we going?" Madigan asked.

"I told you…I have supplies to deliver."

"To the man from the story," Shogun said, realizing now. He looked over at Madigan. Her face had drained of all color.

"Best prepare yourself," Rufus chuckled, spitting a hot wad to the train floor where it joined numerous other strains.

"How's that?"

"For the cold, I mean," he continued, looking away. "You'll see."

The cold did burn. It burned their exposed faces, painfully chapped in the icy wind. They disembarked the train, carefully crossing the slick station floors as they fought against the wind. Rufus fumbled with a set of keys until finally opening the door to the dark ticket booth. He rolled out two snowmobiles, inspecting them before tying on the supplies.

Shogun struggled to keep his focus on Rufus, darting and whizzing through the town at a nauseating speed. If he lost sight of Rufus, Shogun would lose himself and Madigan in that blizzard and that would be that. End of story. Madigan held on to him maybe harder than she needed to. He thought he could feel her racing heartbeat even through the layers of coat between them. And then that mountain. That mountain pulled at him, called for him. *He was coming*, he told it. *Just wait*.

The dust sprite stayed hidden deep behind the collar of Madigan's coat, buried against her neck to keep warm. Madigan watched the remnants of the fallen city pass by, buildings with empty eyes that stared back at her. Doorways that had been open for a long, long time. So long that the outside had crept its way inside and now the two were one in the same. She saw the occasional glint of an animal eye crouched in a corner, hiding from the loud roar of the vehicles. And in the distance, that Snowy North Mountain. A behemoth rising from the frozen ground, looming over the city with a watchful eye.

The mountain terrain grew harsher as they climbed higher and higher. The trails became cluttered with large rocks and thick, strange foliage. Hardy plants built strong to withstand the bitter cold, much less those pesky snowmobiles. The air seemed to thin the higher they climbed. Maybe confiscated by the mountain that now loomed closer than ever, sucking them towards it with the whirl-wind of winds at its command. Madigan couldn't open her eyes. She buried her head in Shogun's back, counting her breaths. In and out. In and out. Again and again. She could feel the hard edge of Sho-gun's axe strapped to his back. It was quiet and dormant. Waiting.

Finally, Rufus stopped. He pulled aside on a nearby clear-ing and motioned for Shogun to do the same. He began to untie the packs of supplies.

"This is it! Can't go any further on the mobiles, too rough!" he shouted above the wind.

Shogun stood up and helped Madigan off the snowmobile. She was stiff and frozen through, not only from the cold but that draining mountain. The elements tried to speak to her but they were a dull voice in the distance, muddled and unclear. Her head was swimming. The group looked down at the empty city below them, silent and still.

Rufus threw two packs of supplies at them. "We're still a ways now, let's go!" He turned and started stomping through the snow, onwards and upwards.

Shogun waited until Rufus had turned then pulled out his axe, strapping on his pack in its place. Madigan reached for her pack but Shogun took it from her. He shook his head and strapped her pack on his back, passing her his axe instead. She stared down at it, surprised by its touch. It stared back at her, just as surprised.

"Keep her safe for me!" Shogun shouted. He looked at Madi-gan then turned and started pushing through the snow after Rufus.

Madigan tucked the axe under her coat. It seemed to mold to the shape of her body, bending and curving along the outline of her rib cage. The axe listened to her heartbeat in that warm space, learning her. Feeding her its own thoughts and agenda. *Fight, fight. Swing, swing. Chop, chop.* The dust sprite peeked down at the axe from its warm place behind Madigan's neck. It shook its head and went back to meditating, pondering the deep pull that emanated from that mountain.

They walked for a long time. They were dark, dim spots in a storm of white. The mountain grew steeper and steeper, stranger and stranger. Shogun watched the trees change from familiar shapes to barren, deformed statues, forever frozen in that snow and wind. They looked at him with blinking eyes, unmoving. The coldness dulled everything. Every thought, every feeling. Rufus charged ahead, unaffected by the thinning air or pressing wind. Shogun watched him. His axe whispered to him from next to Madigan's side. *Be ready for anything.*

Finally, they stopped at a small cave carved into the side of the mountain. Shallow and dark, it dripped with icy water that trickled to the ground, wearing it down drip by drip. Shogun and Madigan gasped for lungful's of air, finally shielded from the wind's grasp. It paced and howled outside the cave, waiting.

Madigan's hands trembled as she drew them out of her coat. The dust sprite emerged as she lit a small fire in her hands, just for her. She called it without thinking, driven by the desire for a small moment of comfort. She closed her eyes and breathed deeply, smelling the aroma of its invisible smoke.

Shogun drank water heavily, rehydrating from the exertion of carrying two packs of supplies and the heat of that heavy coat. He was scalding inside, hot blood running through his veins, his heart pumping harder to get there faster. He watched Madigan's flame. She often fashioned small flames or pools of water, meant for her and the dust sprite and also for Shogun if he cared to look or listen. And sometimes he did care. Sometimes he needed reminded of the place he had always called home. And there and then, that flame was now home.

Rufus stared at Madigan. Shogun watched him observe her carefully. He could have used a tree right about now. There, surrounded in that tomb of rock, Shogun could hear nothing but the growling wind outside. There were thoughts in Rufus' head that Shogun wanted to know. Rufus stepped closer to Madigan, reaching for the flame as if in a trance. She opened her eyes, extinguishing the flame in an instant and looking straight at Rufus. The dust sprite retreated to Madigan's coat again.

"No," she ordered, pointing at Rufus.

Rufus stared back at Madigan. "It's time to go," he said suddenly, grabbing his pack and waiting to make sure they did the same. "We need to get to him before dark."

The afternoon sun was waning outside the cave. It stretched far and thin, fading fast. They could only see quick glimpses of its descent through occasional breaks in the storm. The sun glowed, a hot orb sinking further and further into the ocean of sky. The sun, the moon's distant cousin. Distant and different from each other in many ways. The sun was always outshining her cousin, masking her in bright light so no one could see her until twilight. She was made the queen of darkness without any choice. Always there, forced into silence until the sun completed her sojourn to the other side of the world. Madigan squinted her eyes as the sun turned the snow into fields of glittering diamonds, reflecting even more of her brilliance. Maybe that was why the moon overcompensated so much.

Eventually, the winds began to subside. A slow and gradual change meant to go unnoticed. Now that they could see further than just their hand in front of their face, Shogun spotted a structure in the distance. Carved into the rock, it was a literal stone castle comprised of hollow, glassless windows and doorways of jagged edges. If Shogun blinked he would lose sight of it, as the building seemed to restructure and shift to camouflage itself if given the chance. Madigan slowed her pace. She wasn't sure if the axe was just hot from being strapped next to her sweating body or if there was something else going on. She stared at the castle's dark windows, empty black eye sockets that seemed to know her every move. Without eyes, it had grown other senses. Smart senses that were feeling, listening, and learning them. The dust sprite ventured to the outside of Madigan's coat collar to get a look for itself. It moved up to Madigan's hair. It was going to need to be present for this.

As he approached, Shogun heard a whisper. So faint at first he thought it was just the echo of his heavy breathing in his mind. Then words began to form and he recognized the outline of a tree in the distance. A skeleton of a tree, the bones of a long gone warrior. It reached into the sky with a hundred different barren branches, gnarled and twisted. Shogun had never seen a tree like this. As though it had been burned a dozen times yet it still remained standing. *Try harder next time*, it laughed as it grew taller and taller. Shogun's heart raced as the words became clearer and clearer. If he stood close enough, he could feel it pulsing with thoughts. He tried to soak it up. It knew many things but not the many things Shogun needed.

Rufus walked up the heavy steps with his loud boots. In that silence, the sound reverberated across the stone ground and up the mountain, making the layers of snow creak and crack uneasily. All around them was a sleeping giant of white sleet. Disturb it too much and it may wake up and take you with it. Rufus dropped his pack inside and motioned for Shogun and Madigan. He disappeared into the darkness.

Madigan grabbed Shogun's arm before entering.

"This place," she whispered. "I can't read it. It's...empty to me." The dust sprite tickled her ear. "And the dust sprite feels the same."

Shogun nodded. The tree had given him nothing. It had been one voice talking in a thousand different directions. He wasn't sure if it was just an old, confused tree or a very intelligent tree meaning to mislead him.

"Just be ready," Shogun said, staring past the doorway. Every part of his body was buzzing, anticipating. Ready to snap. Beyond that darkness laid something that was calling for him. Calling for him by name, his name. The voice of the Snowy North Mountain. He had to reach it. There were answers ahead of him. He had to reach it. He stepped through the door into the darkness.

XXVI

THE OLD MAN AND THE CROSSROADS

For one instant, she saw a flash of home behind her eyes. She remembered standing in the rain, in front of her old house with all the old thoughts she knew so well. She heard the sea rolling in the background. The laugh of her little sister beside her. And she remembered a storm that appeared from nowhere. The heavens opened and drained all over her. She had closed her eyes and breathed the heaviest, deepest breaths she had ever taken. She had cried warm tears, moved by the power of it all, closing her eyes to memorize it. And now that day she remembered it, just when she needed it the most.

Across the room from her, Shogun struggled with Rufus, barely visible through the torrential sheet of falling water. They shouted and rolled across the floor, striking and tossing each other through the gathered water that was quickly pooling. Shogun struggled the most, still weighed down by the two packs that were strapped to his back. He shouted out for Madigan above the deafening rain.

But she was trapped, weighed down by the rain. Heavy rain, made of water she had never met before, each drop out to get her. Her soaked clothes became a heavy suit of armor, forcing her down to the ground no matter how much she struggled against it. She reached out to the rain and was only met by screaming. A million screaming voices falling from nowhere. Madigan melted to the ground and gasped for breath as the falling water pummeled her over and over. Her face bled from the coarse rock ground that she was forced against. No matter how much she pleaded, they hit harder and harder. Shogun's axe blazed against her skin, hotter and hotter, trying to scald her into action. *Get me to Shogun. Get me to Shogun. Get me to Shogun.*

They were inside the castle built into the Snowy North Mountain. They had been led there by Rufus, his light raging against the darkness, down hallway after hallway. Then they entered a large room full of evening light and everything changed. Water crashed from the sky like an unleashed waterfall, powerful with freedom. So she had closed her eyes. And remembered.

The dust sprite crawled out from Madigan's drenched hair. She saw it out of the corner of her eye, frail in the falling water.

"Shogun," Madigan struggled between gasps. "The axe..."

The dust sprite disappeared beneath her coat and followed the hot red light emanating from the axe. That heavy coat which now, soaked in water, weighed a hundred times its weight. Madigan gasped as she managed one arm out at a time, freeing enough room for the dust sprite to slowly tug the axe up the body of her coat. Madigan gasped from the strain and the breathlessness of the falling water. She could see the figures of Shogun and Rufus, gray outlines fighting behind the curtain of falling water. Shogun appeared free of his packs now but unaffected by the weight of the water as she was. The dust sprite heaved and pulled, slowly inching the axe free with each beat of Madigan's racing heart.

A loud noise began to reverberate through the air. Madigan's breathing accelerated as a figure rose from a pool of water in the center of the room. An ancient looking figure with skin gray like the approaching twilight sky. She breathed faster and faster, stuck to the ground as the figure stood to full height. The falling water parted for him, quick to get out of his way. The dust sprite pulled harder and harder on Shogun's axe, the movement catching the eye of the old man. He stepped closer, reaching out a wrinkled hand for the axe. He knelt, his face slowly becoming illuminated. Madigan closed her eyes and winced in anticipation. She was completely paralyzed now, every inch of her covered in slick water. Her face burned hot with her own tears. To have come this far and now to end in this place. She wept for everything she had done and not yet done. For everything she had seen and not yet seen. For those she had saved and those she could not.

The rain stopped. There was muffled silence beyond her closed eyelids. She opened her eyes and saw she had developed a shield around herself. Born of her own water, her own teardrops. She could move again, free from the rain that angrily beat against her safe bubble. She could see the hazy outline of the old man, standing above her. He watched, his face a distorted blur.

Madigan grabbed the axe and stumbled through the rain towards Shogun, her shield moving along with her. Rufus had him pinned to the ground, Shogun's face half submerged as the rain greedily added more and more and more water. He saw Madigan approaching, a white orb in the murky gray. Shogun reached out and his axe snapped into his hand, burning so bright that Madigan didn't see the impact that sliced Rufus in two. With a final sigh, the rain dropped hard with one last push. It retreated and drained away, leaving the ground wet and shining in that last evening light.

The room fell silent other than the trickling of water and the heavy gasps for air from Shogun and Madigan. His shoulders limp, the old gray man stared at them. He pointed towards Shogun's axe, its light reflecting in the pools of water scattered across the stone floor. The man began to levitate and Shogun felt a pull on his arm. His axe reacted and resisted. *I won't let you go,* it called to him. Instead of fighting it, Shogun relinquished himself to the old man's tow and felt his feet leave the ground.

Madigan closed her eyes and called to the water. But it was deaf to her there. *We serve another master,* they told her. The wind searched for her but could not find her, they were buried too deep in the caverns of the Snowy North Mountain. She watched helplessly as Shogun drew closer and closer to impacting with the old man until finally they were almost face to face.

Shogun shouted as he strained against the pull on his axe. He struggled to keep his balance, unstable so high in the air. He finally saw the details of the old man's face, features that seemed to melt off his very bones. His eyes were white and blind although they were still drawn to the light of the axe blade, unconcerned with Shogun's presence. He could almost touch it, his bony fingers shaking with anticipation.

Once he was close enough, Shogun kept one hand on his axe and wrapped the other around the old man's neck. The man hacked and lunged forward, furiously trying to shake Shogun off his back. They tumbled through the air and the old man let out a deafening screech as they impacted with the stone ground. Shogun sat up and searched the ground for his axe until he saw trickles of light beneath the old man's robe. He rolled the old man out of the way and found his axe lodged in his back, calling for Shogun. *I won't let you go.*

The old man groaned loudly as Shogun removed the axe. He rolled onto his back as his blood pooled all around him, slowly elevating him off the cold stone ground. Madigan joined Shogun and looked down at the old man, his face now completely revealed. She grimaced at his appearance, painfully deteriorated. He moaned and reached into his robe, pulling out a compass. Shogun dropped to his knees.

"You are the lost wanderer..." Shogun whispered. Somewhere in his heart confirmed it. The man who was the subject of his dreams night after night as a child. The man on the horizon, compass in one hand and sword in the other.

"Find him…" the man whispered, grasping for Shogun's arm. He placed the broken compass in his hand, rusted with age. *"Find them."*

"I will," Shogun promised, closing his fingers around the cool metal of the compass as it began to pulse. "I will."

The cavern began to tremble. Starting from its very foundation, vibrating up the sides of the wall to the ceiling, where large cracks began to form and spread. The old man disappeared into his layers of robe. Rocks began to fall from the ceiling, making the air thick with dusty mist. A loud howl echoed down the hallways, its long fingertips scratching across the rock walls and dragging them down with it. Searching for Madigan, answering her call.

"It's the wind!" Madigan shouted. She ducked out of the way of a falling piece of debris. She had called for it and it had heard her, building as it searched every corner of the cave. "It's too strong!" The dust sprite whizzed around through the air, looking for any signs of escape. Across the room, light began to shine through the cracks in the walls. Small slivers of hope, dusty beams in that dark room.

"There!" Shogun shouted to Madigan, pointing then running towards the beams of light. He ran to the wall and struck it with his axe, putting every last bit of energy into each strike. The axe blade flickered but fought back every time, encouraged as well by the white light that reached for them through the cracking wall.

Madigan stood back as Shogun struck the wall with one last blow, the ring of the axe blade shrill in the air. The rock gave away as a burst of fresh night air flooded the room. Bright beams of light led their way through the murky dust. Madigan crawled outside, her eyes blinded. They were outside, on the other end of the Snowy North Mountain. High above the mountain range that spread out for miles beneath them. The moon was there, glowing in all her glory, jealous of that crystal white Snowy North Mountain that shone without any source at all. The brighter the moon shined, the brighter the mountain reflected it and that infuriated her more than ever before.

Shogun followed behind Madigan, coughing and sputtering out mouthfuls of rocky dust. He breathed in the clean night air, reaching for Madigan and dusting her off. They began to shake in reaction to the freezing temperatures.

"You're alright?" he gasped, inspecting her face. It was streaked with dirty dry tears.

Madigan nodded. Shogun held up the compass for her to inspect. The arms of the compass quivered, delicate heartbeats searching for life as it rested safely in the palm of his hand. It flickered in search of a direction but never found it.

"I can't believe it was really him," Shogun whispered. He looked up across the mountain range and his expression changed. His eyes widened as he motioned for Madigan to look into the horizon.

Two flames had appeared, revealed by the parting mists. Madigan's leading flame, back again to guide them. She stared at them, her heart thumping wildly in her chest. She had not called for two flames but there they were, shining as clear as ever in the distance.

"Why two flames?" Shogun asked, wondering if Madigan had done this herself.

"A crossroads," Madigan replied, her voice cracking.

Shogun shook his head. "No. We're not splitting up."

"We have to."

"No, we'll try one direction and if it's wrong, we'll go back and try the next."

"There's no time."

"Yes, there is."

"No!" Madigan began to sob. "Do you want to end up like him?"

Shogun was silent. He looked down at his axe, the light slowly dimming from the blade as it fell into a quiet slumber, no longer needed. He had seen a reflection of himself in the old man's blank eyes. A man with his own enchanted object, forever searching for the answer that eluded him. The man of his childhood dreams was now a potential reality.

"You know I'm right," Madigan whispered.

Dust continued to escape out of the cracked hole in the wall. The rumbling inside the room dulled to a slow roll as the wind calmed itself, repeating over and over that Madigan was safe, *Madigan was safe*. But she was shaking in that freezing night air, wet and numb. Her heart thumped madly, deeply. She had a thousand words to say but she couldn't quite say them. The moon watched from her perch in the sky, for once trying not to pry.

A horn echoed through the silent night snow. Loud and obnoxious, blaring louder and louder, over and over. Headlights revealed a vehicle haphazardly making its way across the terrain, getting caught in drifts but still managing to fight its way through. The dust sprite came to Madigan's shoulders, beaming brightly and excitedly. It was a bus, a familiar bus, filled with its friends and family it had missed so much. The dust sprite's home.

"Meadowsweet?" Shogun said, shaking his head in slow disbelief. He watched as the bus fought harder and harder across the snow, chugging closer and closer, horn blaring. Shogun raised his hand in recognition and the bus stopped, revving its engine for him impatiently.

"I guess that's your ride," Madigan said hoarsely. Her eyes burned with bitter tears.

"No, we're going together," Shogun insisted again in as firm of a tone as he could muster, thinking it would convince her.

"Take the dust sprite," Madigan reached for the dust sprite and cupped it in her hand. "You can go home," she whispered. "Go home." The dust sprite flickered in protest but retreated to Shogun's pocket, peeking over the edge to look at her.

Meadowsweet honked again and again for him. Shogun couldn't even look in Madigan's eyes, it caused a pain like he had never experienced before. "I can't...I can't do this without you," he said finally. His heart thumped madly, deeply. He had a thousand words to say but he couldn't quite say them.

"Choose your flame," Madigan said firmly, looking away so he couldn't see the tears in her eyes.

"No."

"Choose it!"

Shogun sighed heavily, clenching his jaw hard. He pointed to one of the flames, the one that kept drawing his attention over and over. When he looked back, Madigan was gone.

XXVII

THE NORTH SEA

"Cheer up, honeykins. I don't want to see that sour look on such a pretty little face."

Shogun looked up darkly at Meadowsweet's reflection in the rear view mirror. She winked at him and grinned, bells ringing in the distance. He turned his head and went back to staring out the window, the dust sprite joining him beside the milky glass. They were watching the flame, hanging stationary in the sky. A strange sort of sun in the early morning sky, a ball of crackling heat. It was waiting for him to catch up, boldly blazing brighter and brighter as he drew nearer and nearer. Shogun felt its pull inside his chest, as though he was caught in the flame's centrifugal force.

Meadowsweet sighed loudly. She shifted gears on the bus and it picked up speed. "You and your one track mind! I thought you and I could catch up a bit, *but no*, you just want to look out the window. What a dud. We'll get there soon enough, don't get your britches in a bunch!"

The dust sprite pulsed a low glow. A sad, aching glow. One by one, a few of its family members would come out to check on it, but they knew to leave well enough alone. Shogun wasn't sure how to comfort the dust sprite as he wasn't sure how to comfort himself, either. A part of him had gone missing and he didn't know if he would see her ever again.

They had descended from the Snowy North Mountain rather quickly, partly because of Meadowsweet's reckless driving and partly because that seemed to be the design of the Snowy North Mountain. Get in quick and get out the same way. The flame flickered through the arms of a few straggly trees, outcasts of the Central Forest. Strange, deformed creatures, unsure of where they belonged. They were rooted in this harsh land, where bitter winds stripped them slowly of their bark. Where snow stopped any hope of leaves or other life. They were doomed to be frozen statues, that was their fate, and they accepted it.

"Where do you think it is?" Shogun called to Meadowsweet above the roar of the loud engine, keeping his eyes on the flame.

Meadowsweet squinted as she peered out her side window. She put on a pair of dusty glasses and squinted again. "Right smack over the North Sea, if you ask me." She returned her attention to the road. "Oh, this road, always twisting and turning," Meadowsweet mumbled to herself, simultaneously driving and checking her reflection in the mirror. The bus swerved as she struggled to keep it on course.

"The North Sea..." Shogun whispered to the dust sprite. It couldn't be right.

"The most pointless sea, if you ask me! But if that's where your little flame has run off to, then we'll get there, eventually." Meadowsweet cursed again at the twisty road. "This damn road! Worse design I've ever seen, built into the damn mountain, makes no sense, *tsk tsk.*"

"How long until we get there?"

"Oh, awhile. Best get comfortable."

"We need to get there fast."

"Oh, demanding now, are we? And who saved you off that frozen mountain, hm?"

"I'm sorry, I just…"

"You know, I've just about had it, so stop your bellyaching!" Meadowsweet shouted back to Shogun. "We're gonna take a shortcut, who needs this damn road, anyway!"

Before Shogun could reply, Meadowsweet spun the steering wheel with all the might of her short arms. The bus shot over the edge of the road and down the rocky terrain, knocking down small trees and other obstacles in its way. Shogun went flying out of his seat across the bus, only able to make out flashes of light from where he laid on the ground, head spinning. He could hear branches snapping and rocks knocking against the side of the sliding bus.

"Hold on, laddie!" Meadowsweet hollered. She laughed and began honking the horn.

Finally, the bus slid to a stop. A gradual, exhausted stop. Shogun was able to stand with the help of a nearby seat to steady himself.

"Was that really necessary?" he shouted, cradling his aching head.

Another dramatic sigh from Meadowsweet. She turned around in her chair and rolled her eyes. "First, I'm not going fast enough and then I'm going too fast! Picky, picky!" She returned to the steering wheel and tried turning over the engine. It ticked in response. "Oh boy, now you've done it. Give me a second here, honey buns."

Shogun crawled over to the window. The dust sprite was still there, seemingly unaffected by the recent turn of events. It was watching the flame which was now significantly closer than before. So close that Shogun was sure this was the cause of the heaviness in his head. He could almost hear the flame crackling, but then he realized it was another sound he heard. The North Sea. They were on the beach of the North Sea.

"You did it!" Shogun called out, almost hysterically. The flame burned so close that it cast a red glow on the pale sands.

"Well, not quite, deary. Still trying...to get...this bus...there!" Meadowsweet whooped triumphantly as the bus engine fired to a start. A huge cloud of black smoke billowed behind them.

"Onward!" Meadowsweet charged, navigating the bus across the firm sand.

Shogun joined her at the front of the bus. She was wearing driving goggles to keep out any wayward sand that snuck in through the cracked windshield. The flame grew closer and closer and the pit in Shogun's stomach grew larger and larger. He could not deny it any longer. The flame was hovering above the sea. Hanging without threads or support, floating hotly, warming the water below it.

"I chose the wrong flame," he admitted sourly. "This should have been for Madigan, not me."

"Oh, you think so, eh?" Meadowsweet chortled.

"I don't know anything about this!"

"And what is *this?*"

"The sea. The ocean. The water. Any of it!"

"Maybe you should wonder if that's the point," Meadowsweet mumbled as she shrugged. "Just sayin'."

Shogun returned to his seat. The dust sprite was still there, motionless. So still that Shogun wondered if it was dead, but then it would occasionally offer a flicker of a quiet glow. Outside the window, the flame was watching the little bus that raced towards it across the beach. Shogun's axe began to burn. Hot pulses, synchronizing with each of his breaths. Faster and faster. He closed his eyes but that hot orb was still there, clear as ever beneath his eyelids. The dust sprite floated to Shogun's clenched hands. It rested there and closed its eyes, too.

The bus lurched to a halt. "Last stop!" Meadowsweet called out in an official tone, reaching over and opening the door. A burst of cold wind rushed in. She cursed and opened it just a crack instead. Shogun stood up and walked down the bus for the last time.

"Thank you," Shogun told Meadowsweet. "Again."

"Good luck, lover," Meadowsweet whispered through a grin. She nodded her head. "I'd tip my hat to you, if I had one."

Shogun descended the rickety bus steps. The cold air was strong and tried to push him around brutishly. With a honk of her horn, Meadowsweet was gone, cutting back across the beach and disappearing into the hills. In front of him, the sea tossed and the giant flame peered down at him. He wasn't sure what he expecting after so long of chasing it down. But he wasn't expecting this.

He watched the ocean lap at the sand at a steady rate, in and out. A heartbeat without end, never faltering. On the horizon, Shogun began to make out a small craft. A boat, he believed, bobbing up and down with each rolling wave. He waited to see if it would come closer to where he stood on the sand, but it never budged as though anchored to the ocean floor, somewhere deep down there. Shogun felt his throat tighten as he slowly removed his boots and coat and stripped down to his pants and undershirt. That deep down there was what he was worried about. He reached back and made sure his axe was firmly attached for the ride. His back was already moist, as though his axe was perspiring with him.

Step by step, Shogun entered the roaring sea. He looked over his shoulder at the dust sprite who hesitantly remained on the beach, his cheerleader from the sidelines. The salty water stung and cleansed his skin, burning his eyes with every splash. These waves were like nothing he had ever experienced. Each one a wild animal, Shogun had to wrestle with it before it tackled him down. Trying to drag him down, down, down to those unknown depths that Shogun was fine to leave unknown. He fought against the choppy water, sloppily swimming towards the small boat in the distance. The flame cracked and hissed above his head, sizzling as ocean sprays dared to jump up and try to touch it. *I will strike you down.* Don't touch, just listen. I will strike you down.

His arms began to grow tired by the time Shogun realized there was someone in the craft. "Hey!" he shouted above the crashing of the waves. Shogun disappeared under for a moment then resurfaced again. He was starting to get the hang of it. He only had a few more moments until the next wave tried to drag him down with it. "Hey, you!"

The figure on the boat did not respond. The closer he got, Shogun realized it was a man. He kept his back to Shogun.

"Hey! Need some help here!" Shogun called again. His arms were burning now, half from strain and half from inexperience. The further he swam out to sea, the wilder the water grew. Untamed beasts, free to follow their own will without the chiding glances from the shore.

Shogun found he was disappearing below the water's surface longer and longer each time. That burning flame became further and further away and with it, air. Shogun knew he was getting closer, but he never seemed to be quite in reach of the craft. The strange silence below the water began to lull him with a soft, whispering song. His axe burned hot to keep him alert.

Suddenly, Shogun became trapped. His arms and legs were entangled in a net, invisible until too late. It trapped him without pain, almost apologetically, but kept him tight within its cage. He could only float, lost in the net's silky embrace. He couldn't even reach back for his axe, which burned and cursed his name to fight back. The corners of his eyes began to go black when Shogun finally felt a tug on the nets. He was above surface and dropped into the boat in one fluid motion.

As he coughed up lungful's of water, Shogun's eyes began to focus on the figure in front of him. A middle-aged man, with broad shoulders and eyes as bright as stars shining out from behind his dark shaggy hair. The man looked familiar to Shogun but he didn't know why.

"Thank you," he managed between breaths. Shogun looked up at the flame. It was right over his head now.

The man nodded his head and began to hum. It seemed as though he was looking right through Shogun or right over his head. Past him, into the horizon and maybe far beyond it. He closed his eyes and began to gather the nets in his rugged hands, nodding and singing softly to himself.

> *A fire burns across the sea.*
> *I will call your name and you will come to me.*
> *And you will sleep and dream of the night.*
> *And dream of me.*
>
> *A fire burns across the sea.*
> *Light my way over the misty trees.*
> *Far across the fields, they will hear my voice.*
> *If I listen, I will see.*
>
> *A fire burns across the sea.*
> *Watching and wishing, waiting for thee.*

The man sang quietly, as though only to himself and the nets that he wove in his hands, thread over thread, verse after verse. Shogun watched him. Now he recognized him. Now he knew this voice. Echoing back from the furthest corners of his mind, from the place that cherishes only the best of childhood memories. It was Jacob, Madigan's father. A dead man there in the flesh, but not really. Not really there, just skin and bones and eyes that shone with a strange light. He seemed unaware that Shogun was present or maybe didn't care.

The sea had grown significantly calmer. The small boat rocked back and forth softly, only bumping them when the occasional swell would come their way and could not be avoided. Jacob continued to smile and sing to himself, knotting and threading and kneading the silky nets between his fingers. Occasionally a fish would plop into the boat and Jacob would nod appreciatively but kept weaving.

"I dreamed of a girl, once," Jacob began to whisper to himself. "And she was beautiful. And she was my girl. And she would change everything."

Shogun looked around to see if there was anyone he was talking to. There was just the flat expanse of sea everywhere he looked.

Now Jacob was wiping tears from his dark eyes with the backs of his hands, still weaving. The wind began to pick up as he softly wept, smiling to himself. "And she will change everything."

In the distance, a large dark cloud began to form. Shogun watched it manifest across the sea, growing from a small speck into a pillar of shadows. The once flat waters were now becoming choppy in the swirling winds. When he looked back, Jacob was staring right at him with his empty, bright eyes. He held out the finished net, neatly wrapped and gleaming.

"Take care of her, she is my light in that darkness," Jacob whispered, leaning forward. The wind whipped his hair wildly, urging him on.

Shogun met his gaze and nodded. He took the net. It was freezing to the touch but softer than anything he had ever felt before. Jacob sighed and looked over at the dark cloud that approached faster and faster. Shogun had lost sight of the leading flame, now engulfed by the sudden storm. He tucked the net under his shirt and held onto the edges of the rocking boat, trying to see through the sprays of water. Jacob stood up and climbed onto the edge. He looked back at Shogun and smiled.

"I knew your father, once! The man he was before!" Jacob called over the wind. He balanced precariously on the edge of the boat. He laughed and shook his head. "A good man, that Paddie Saban. A good man that I called my friend! You'll meet him again, one day!"

And then he was gone. Enveloped by the dark cloud without a sound, swallowed by the silent storm. It floated in front of Shogun's face, meeting his gaze with electricity. *You can look, but don't touch.* Within its spinning airways, Shogun heard a thousand voices whispering. He inched to the far edge of the boat, making sure to avoid any wispy tendrils. Then it was gone, continuing its journey across the water without reflection. In a hurried gust, the wind charged after it, causing the boat to capsize. Before he could even take a breath, there was a flash of light and rushing water and Shogun was submerged. He swam to the best of his abilities. This experience was making him prefer the forest more and more.

Exhausted, Shogun dragged himself back onto the beach. He had no idea how much time had passed, but now thin evening light stretched across the expanse above the sea. Lying on the wet sand, he reached back and made sure his axe was still there. It was cold and traumatized by the harsh salt water, but present and accounted for. Shogun sat up and pulled the silky net out from beneath his shirt. He wasn't sure what he was looking at but it was beautiful. Glistening milky white in that evening light, tough yet almost melting between his fingertips. He knew one thing for sure. This was no ordinary net.

Forcing himself to stand up, Shogun stumbled towards the remainder of his clothes that he had dumped on the sand. The dust sprite whizzed around his head, glowing brightly and settling into Shogun's hair. Finding it soaking wet, it returned back to his dry jacket but darted back into the air. It caught sight of a figure in the distance and flashed for Shogun's attention. There was a flame, flickering faintly on the horizon. If not for its low position, the flame could have easily been mistaken for an early evening star. Shogun's axe burned to attention.

"I see it," Shogun assured them. "I see it."

XXVIII

THE HOUSE OF GHOSTS

It was whispering her name, she was sure of it. There in that darkness, the moon beside her, a voice called for her. Her leading flame hung above her head, a heavy inferno, cracking and licking at the air. It almost hurt her eyes to look at it. Almost. Because in its hot depths, Madigan saw the memory of a little girl and her father, building a fire. Back on Shrunken Hollow Road a long, long time ago.

The moon watched the flame from behind a veil of clouds. She was unsure of this other floating object, not quite celestial but not quite of the firmament either. It intrigued her, this mindless creature sent on a quest to find an unknown destination. That was its only purpose. Its only reason for creation. To guide and lead, then stop. Now it stood like a solemn sentry at the entrance of the forest, casting a warm glow outside the dark woods. This is it. *You asked and I have led you here.*

Yes, something was calling for her. Madigan's throat clenched. She had walked a long way, trekking towards her flame without stopping for food or rest. She was fixated on it, obsessed. Unable to eat or sleep due to a lack of appetite and a restless mind. Slowly, that flame grew bigger and bigger and this all became more and more real. Why her flame had led her to this dark forest, at this entrance, on this starry night, she didn't know. But eyes glowed within the woods, watching her next move. Pacing, calling for her to make it.

The moon cast a light down into the woods, snooping around to see if the coast was clear. She shrugged her gossamer shoulders as she reported seeing nothing out of the ordinary. *But what was ordinary to a moon*, Madigan wanted to clarify. The moon scoffed and pulled her veil completely over her head, disappearing from sight for an appropriately moody amount of time.

Slowly, the flame began to dim. Subtly changing, quieter and quieter, until it was just a tiny ember. Like a seed, dormant and waiting to be reawakened. Madigan was left in complete darkness. Every sound was amplified in that stillness meant for her. Her shaking breath made her heart race even more. She clung to every star above her head as her only points of light in the thick black. Now, in that darkness, she was able to see into the forest. Through the trees, a small light shone in a window, fragile and quiet. It wasn't a candle, but a steady light. A dining room light mounted on the ceiling. She entered the forest and walked towards it. *Because it was now or never*, the moon chided over her shoulder.

This place was familiar but slightly off, skewed in the strange, dull light. As she grew closer to the house, she finally recognized its shape. It was Shogun's house. Roland's house. Paddie's house. Although not dark as it was at the end. It was the house she remembered from her childhood, where there was laughter and light. Madigan stepped closer to the building, the pine needles crunching beneath her feet. She paused and finally summoned the nerve to look through the milky window.

She could see no one in the house but it was without a doubt Shogun's old home. She recognized the couch and the dining room table and the awful wallpaper. There were the sliding glass doors that led to the back of the house. That prized area, where they practiced their foolery and stood and stared at their trees with their morning coffee. Brought out chairs and sat and stared at the trees some more. Watching, listening, learning.

Through the sliding glass doors, she could see movement. Moving back and forth, a dull figure through the foggy glass. A voice that was loud and full of laughter. The tightness in her throat returned, there in that little circle of light through the window glass. Surrounded by the dark forest, the little remaining ember of her flame long gone from sight. Above Madigan's head, the night sky was so thick even the moon couldn't penetrate it. She took a big breath and willed herself to leave the safety of the window light.

Madigan slowly entered through the front door. She was met by the strong odor of woods in that house, stronger even than outdoors. The floor creaked beneath her feet. She shuddered at the memory of her last encounter with this place. As she entered the dining room, she caught the eye of Paddie. He was standing at the kitchen counter, making a sandwich. He stopped and stared at her. This was a younger Paddie and it stunned her to see the resemblance with Shogun. He stared at her for a few more heartbeats but said nothing, returning to his sandwich.

Without delay, she rushed out the sliding glass doors. Roland was on the back concrete patio, swashbuckling with his sword back and forth. He was so entranced he didn't see Madigan for several minutes. She watched him perform his dance of swords, moving smoothly from one move to the next. This Roland was still old, as though he had always been old, right from the start.

Something caused him to break concentration and Roland finally noticed Madigan, huddled up beneath the eaves of the house. He grinned ear to ear.

"Ah! There you are!" he shouted louder than necessary. "Come on, come on, now! Where have you been, Charlotte Madigan?"

"I..." Madigan stammered, looking around.

"I've been waiting for you! Come on!" Roland motioned for her to stand next to him. He reached over and readied a rope that was hanging from one of the nearby trees.

Madigan walked towards him slowly, hesitant to deny anything to this dream. Because this was a dream, it had to be. Wasn't it? She stood next to Roland and felt his cold energy floating towards her sweaty skin. It was Roland, but not Roland. His face seemed fuzzy to Madigan, but maybe it was because she was afraid to look too closely.

Roland carefully tied the rope around her waist. He mumbled to himself as he tested the rope, nodding and testing it again. Paddie opened the sliding glass door and came to watch, slowly chewing his sandwich. He made Madigan uncomfortable as he stared at her, as though searching to remember how he knew her. One bite after another, he seemed to get closer and closer to remembering.

"Alright...there we are. Perfect. Ready?" Roland announced, sheathing his sword and making one last yank on the thick rope.

"Ready to... what?" Madigan stammered.

"To fly!"

With a sudden jerk, she was up in the air. The force knocked the air out from her lungs. Instantly, she was off the ground and within the treetops. Madigan gasped and reached out for the nearest tree, wrapping her body around its firm trunk. Roland laughed from down on the ground. She could barely make him out through the thick limbs.

"Thatta girl! Now, climb! Climb!" he urged. Paddie had joined him now at the base of the tree, almost done with his sandwich.

Once Madigan had calmed her breath, she dared to look up above her. Peeking through the very tops of the trees was bright sky. The moon was there, peering down into the strange little forest but unable to find Madigan in that dense land of limbs. So she moved on, floating effortlessly through the sky, unconcerned with looking too closely.

Roland chanted encouraging words from below, telling her to climb, climb, climb. So she tried, branch by branch. Step by step. Soon, Roland's chants grew fainter and fainter. She had to talk herself through each movement. She had never climbed a tree, not once in her life. Neither had her sister or brother or mother or father and fairly sure no one else before her, either. This was no place for her, high in the thin air, further and further away from the sea floor. But she kept climbing until soon she was so high that the wind whipped the exposed treetops. It was a wild place, there in the high air without any limbs to slow down the wind. It was the top of the world for those trees, there was nothing any higher.

Now in the windy open air, Madigan could breathe. She swallowed long, deep lungful's of it, tasting slightly of the faraway salt water. The night sky was alive with stars, many more visible from this tall vantage point. The moon had still not spotted her as she casually made her rounds above the little forest. But in the distance a flame blazed, strong and bright as ever. The little ember was gone, finally released to fade away and allow this new flame to emerge. It caught her eye and summoned to Madigan.

Much more quickly than her ascension, Madigan climbed back down the sturdy tree. Its branches whisked against her face, trying to get a glimpse inside this girl of the sea. She was so guarded, her exterior was tougher than any of them. But beneath her skin was rushing blood and passion and feelings they would never have expected. It caught the tree off guard so it called to the next level of branches to touch her face and so on and so forth. Each level learned something new. Each branch discovered something different.

She dropped to the ground ungraciously, panting in relief at the touch of firm ground. Madigan didn't realize how tightly she had been breathing, as though she needed to conserve her oxygen being that high off the ground. By the time her head stopped swimming, Madigan realized that Roland was gone.

His sword was lying on the ground, shining in the dim light of the porch light. It was an old sword, long and gray. It had seen many places and many faces, always at Roland's side. Madigan struggled with the rope around her waist, finally freeing herself. She reached down and picked up the sword, a shrill metallic sound ringing out as it dragged against the concrete patio.

It was then that she noticed Paddie, still standing by the sliding glass door, watching. He stared at her, blinking slowly and deliberately. She met his gaze but it chilled her. His eyes were black, as though they were just holes in his head. He looked down at Roland's sword but didn't move.

Slowly, Madigan walked around Paddie. Making a wide arc, she held the sword up against her body, telling herself she could use it if she needed to. She would use it she had to. And part of her wanted to. She kept Paddie's gaze, watching for any flinches. But he didn't move besides following her with his eyes, dark and steady. Maybe it would be mercy to drive the sword through him right now and free him of this place. So she walked away, leaving him there in that place between the living and the dead.

Once she had circled to the front of the house, Madigan broke into a run. She ran faster than she had before, letting her fear break free and give her wings. She looked back once and saw the light inside the house slowly dimming to darkness, Paddie's figure silhouetted in front of the window. She ran even faster, back to the entrance of the forest, Roland's heavy sword wrapped in her arms.

She collapsed to the ground outside the forest, recapturing her breath in the early dawn. She studied Roland's sword. She had seen it before but never this close. It hummed with something deep within. Madigan tied the sword to her back the best she could. Over her shoulder, the leading flame burned for her. Calling one last time.

XXIX

THE EASTERN SHRINE

The eastern coastline was a strange place that most found uninhabitable. The soil was dry and lifeless, only the coarse coastal grasses found a way to survive there. When the storms came, they came intense. Rain fell more in sheets than droplets. Wind blew more in gusts than a breeze. When summer came it burned hot and long, blistering the ground relentlessly. When winter came it brought dampness that was bitterly cold. The kind of cold that took up residence in a person's joints and tried to freeze them from the inside out. The land had been abandoned a long time ago but one structure remained. A shrine left to deteriorate but instead it grew. And watched. And listened.

It shined beneath the glary sky. Shogun stared at it from the hilltop, the dust sprite on his shoulder. The shrine's large golden dome was almost blinding as it reflected the light from above and scattered it tenfold. The leading flame was burning furiously above it, a passionate dance of heat reflected in the dome's smooth surface. The milky white stucco of the shrine's columns were pristine from years and years of the salty wind's cleansing touch, scrubbing it clean. The windows consisted of long rectangle frames filled with thick, cold glass. Thick and cold like the sea that rolled and whispered behind it.

Everything was quiet, Shogun noticed it immediately. As though at this place, the trees were just trees and that is all. It had taken him a long time to reach this flame. Longer than he wanted or intended. He walked with his head down, restricting himself from his thoughts. Just walk, don't listen. When he realized how close he was, he walked without stopping. He knew he was close when the heat from the flame licked at his skin even from a distance, an unquenchable inferno burning stronger and stronger with each passing second. He looked down at his dry, dirty hands. He barely recognized this person he had become. His axe was silent on his back, lost in a dream.

The dust sprite left his shoulder in a flash. Shogun was focused on the heat from the flame. It was burning so furiously that he began to wonder how he would get close enough to the building to even enter it. He was about to drop to the ground for a rest when he heard footsteps. Slow, heavy steps through the grass. The flame raged now, uncontrollable and ready to burst. Madigan was walking up the hill, the dust sprite nestled against her tan neck. *Home again.*

Madigan saw Shogun and paused, unsure how to react. Inside, she was half crying, half laughing in relief when she saw him. They made it. This was it. They survived. Madigan looked at him with a crooked smile. He was just as haggard looking as her. Maybe just as terrified, too. He grabbed her hand as she took the last few steps and pulled her against him.

"I...have something for you," Shogun said, his voice broken. He realized it had been a long time since he'd spoken to anyone. The dust sprite didn't count. He shuffled through his coat pockets and pulled out Jacob's net. Still just as soft as that first moment he drew it from the North Sea's waters, now rolled into a messy ball after being stuffed in Shogun's pocket for so long.

Madigan reached for the nets carefully. Her fingers trembled as she examined each thread, swallowing hard as she recognized every fiber. She felt the tears as she buried her face in their soft lace and smelled a mixture of her father's soap and the fresh ocean air from home. She smiled and breathed again. *Home.* Without another thought, she unraveled the nets and let them catch air. They glowed as the beating sun reflected off each strand.

"Thank you..." she whispered and nodded, gathering the net and folding it neatly. She held it against her chest and let her heart beat next to it. For a moment, she thought she felt another heart beating back. She looked up at Shogun, turning around to reveal Roland's sword strapped to her back.

"I'm ready to be done with this thing," she said, half serious.

"It can't be..." Shogun whispered, carefully removing his grandfather's sword from her back. Madigan sighed and straightened up now that she was free from its weight.

Shogun tossed the sword between his hands. It wasn't as heavy as he remembered from his childhood. In fact, it was just right. It fit perfectly in his palm when his fingers were clasped around it, as though a mold had been created just in his hand's likeness. His grandfather's sword was now his. That sword he had been allowed to only look at and not touch. Maybe his grandfather knew how familiar it would feel to him. Maybe he knew what path this sword could take him down. Shogun studied every detail on the weapon's hilt, lines once blurry memories were now real and tangible. He shook his head and looked at Madigan. "Amazing," he whispered.

Shogun jerked as his axe burned ferociously on his back. He dropped the sword and clawed the axe off his skin with a shout. It was white hot, steam sizzling off the sharpened blade. He dropped it to the ground next to the sword, where the axe singed the grass. In turn, Roland's sword began to smoke in recognition of Shogun's axe. With a loud ring of metal, the sword and axe clanged together

as though magnetized. They burned orange like lava and meld-
ed together, the axe layered atop the sword. Separate yet together.
Different but the same. Then the hot light of the weapon burned
down until finally cool to the touch. Shogun picked it up in his
hands and examined it carefully. "Amazing," he repeated.

The flame hanging over the shrine died out with a long,
drawn pillar of smoke. Evaporating into the atmosphere, finally finished with the task commissioned by Madigan a long
time ago. They watched the flame disappear, its ghost lingering
a bit longer to make sure that Shogun and Madigan figured
out the final step. It wanted to see this part for itself after all
this anticipation. Maybe Shogun saw its outline against the
clouds because something made him think.

Shogun tucked the sword into his belt and pulled out the broken compass. He studied the old and intricate design as he had
a hundred times before. He pressed the broken glass face of the
compass with his finger and another layer popped open. The corner of a piece of paper peeked out from there. Shogun met Madigan's gaze and she carefully tugged on the paper until it was in her
hands. The ghost of the flame faded away, finally satisfied.

The paper was delicate and stained with age. She opened it
and they stared down at a barely visible drawing. Rushed and
desperate, as though to capture a quick glimpse of a shape. As
though to capture a moment from a dream. Madigan held the
paper up to the sunset and matched the drawing to the outline of the shrine. Hairs stood on the back of her neck as she
lowered it to look at Shogun. He was staring at the shrine. The
setting sun had revealed a faint light flickering inside the building beyond the cold, thick windows. And along with that light,
there was movement. He removed the sword from his belt.

"Can we do this?" she whispered, partly to herself. The wind
whipped her hair wildly, trying to tell her a thousand things. But
in that place, she had no way of hearing them.

"Yes," Shogun replied. But sweat was starting to bead on his forehead and his breaths looked controlled and heavy. His heart raced so wildly against his ribcage he thought for sure, this time, it would find a way to beat free.

Now the sun had set completely, leaving the last faint remainder of the day. In that light, magic could happen. A strange world between light and darkness, where neither the sun or moon reigned. This was it. This was the time. Without another word, Shogun and Madigan began their descent towards the shrine. The tall grasses pulled at them, warning them wordlessly. The dust sprite shivered from the nape of Madigan's neck. *This was the time. This was it.*

Approaching slowly, Shogun led the way along the side of the shrine. They slid beneath the windows, Madigan's hand pressed against the rough stucco. It felt real, felt tangible. Part of her had imagined the entire building was an illusion. They could still identify movement within by the shadows cast on the hillside. Madigan pulled her hand away when a low groan echoed from inside the shrine, vibrating through the exterior walls. She had never heard a sound like that before. It seemed to search out every fear she had inside and shake it up, bigger and bigger until all her fears towered over her. Madigan covered her mouth to keep from screaming and felt herself begin to blackout.

Shogun reached out and grabbed her arm. He gripped it a bit harder than he would have, strengthened by the adrenaline pumping through him. He had heard it, too. Felt it, too. He held his sword so hard that he felt the bones of his fingers threatening to dislocate.

"Hold on," he whispered to her. "Hold on."

The shrine had no door, just a giant entrance of crumbling stone. After several minutes passed without any sound or sign of movement within, Shogun and Madigan crept up to its threshold. Looking around the corner, Shogun took a quick look inside. He turned back.

"I don't see anything," he reported to Madigan quietly. "There's a large room. It's dark, a few lights are lit." For the briefest, flicker of a moment, he wondered if he had imagined everything he had seen and heard. Maybe figments of his imagination. It was just an old, creepy building, that's all. But down in his hand, his sword was telling him otherwise. A low moan emanated through the entrance and Shogun bowed his head. It was real.

Madigan had closed her eyes, small tears streaming down her face. This fear was crushing her from inside. She thought she had been afraid before. She thought she had seen darkness, but this was different. The dust sprite had buried into her hair, reassuring her. Reminding her of why they were here. And saying goodbye.

"No!" Madigan whispered loudly, her eyes popping open. She reached out but the dust sprite avoided her grasp and shot inside the shrine. Shogun held Madigan back as an explosion of light burst inside, followed by a loud roar. He held her tight, in front of his face.

"Madigan!" he shouted above the noise. "Now!"

She nodded, wiping away the last of her tears. In their wake, her eyes were flashing.

Inside, the room was filled with a dark cloud of a hundred voices. Remnants of light from the dust sprite's charge filtered through the air. The cloud had no real form, just a darkness that had seeped into every crevice of the shrine and manifested there. Shogun had seen this cloud before, or something like it. On the boat in the North Sea, it had swallowed the ghost of Madigan's father. The cloud gathered itself up into a giant pillar of darkness and shrieked. Shogun's sword glowed to the point of almost blinding. The darkness shrieked even louder then evaporated.

Then it was quiet. Madigan clung to Shogun's back, their breathing loud and labored in the still, hot air. The room was a hazy blur. The last remaining light from the setting sun was about to leave them.

"I like your sword," a voice called from the thick black. "Can it be mine?"

Shogun looked around. He couldn't see anything beyond the white of his sword. Madigan gripped his back harder and harder. "It belongs to me," he answered.

"Hmm," the voice murmured. "Not for long, I think."

Another loud roar blasted through the chamber, knocking Shogun and Madigan backwards. They heard rustling as the creature moved around the room. It began to groan and tick like a clock.

"So tired…so tired…so tired of you!" it shrieked, causing Shogun's sword to leap in brightness. It revealed the dark cloud gathered in the corner, rising higher and higher.

Madigan looked down as she felt a warmth on her stomach. She had tucked her father's nets beneath her shirt for safe keeping but now they were revealing themselves, glowing and shimmering like diamonds.

"I can catch it," Madigan quickly whispered into Shogun's ear. He turned to meet Madigan's gaze. "Draw it out and I can catch it."

Without another word they separated and Madigan disappeared into the darkness. Shogun waited a beat before holding up his sword.

"Where are you?" he shouted, stepping back into a striking stance.

Immediately the darkness shrieked again, rattling the windows and causing debris to crumble from the ceiling. Through the falling dust, Shogun could see the creature begin to swirl.

"Ready to join the others?" a voice screamed.

A burst of wind knocked Shogun across the ground, slamming him against the hard wall of the shrine. The impact caused him to drop his sword along the way. The dark cloud rose up until it formed a tall tower made of particles continuously changing shape. It charged towards the sword that was left vulnerable in the middle of the cold floor. Shogun shouted and stumbled towards his sword, only just within his reach.

A net of light soared through the air. It seemed to stretch and expand, a thousand fibers woven together as one, gathering the dark particles beneath its interlocking pathways. The creature shrieked, pushing desperately against the barrier of light. The shrine began to shake violently, as though the net was purging darkness out of every corner. The creature shrunk into a twisted and shriveled old man, covered in a blanket of liquid gold. He inhaled laboriously before he raised his crooked neck.

"I see," he sighed, holding up his arms to study the golden net that dripped off him, trapping him. "You have me, now."

Madigan joined Shogun, helping him stand from the ground. She stared, mesmerized by what she had done. Her father's net had captured it, woven in the darkness to trap the darkness.

"But it's no concern," the old man continued. "You will free me."

Shogun reached down and snatched his sword. "I doubt that."

The creature laughed. "I am sure of it. I have something you want."

He reached his thin arms into the air, the heavy golden fibers of the net clanking together. The chamber of the shrine filled with light and beside him, an apparition began to form. Outlines of shapes appeared, swirling and sharpening until they became clear.

Madigan gripped Shogun's shoulder. She would have recognized her sister's small frame anywhere. Beside Sara, her mother and brother began to form until finally, Jacob. They stood in a strange, broken haze, eyes dull and blank. There but not there. Real but not real. She saw on Shogun's face that he was seeing something similar.

"What do you see?" she whispered.

"My grandfather and father," Shogun answered, swallowing hard. "And my mother."

They stared at him, pleadingly he thought. Was it possible? Shogun only knew the image of his mother from pictures, but this was her, as in the flesh as he had ever seen her. She was beautiful. Roland looked just the same, puffing away at his pipe. Paddie had an axe in his hand. A younger Paddie, strong and intense. A Paddie before the darkness took him.

"I told you," the creature jeered, looking between them from beneath his robe of golden net. "I *do* have something you want."

Shogun and Madigan both faltered. Madigan felt her breath catch in her throat. She wanted to run straight for them.

"Do I bring them back?" The creature rattled his golden chains at them. "You know what to do...set me free."

"Bring them back..." Shogun repeated. He was staring into the eyes of his father, someone he recognized but from a very long time ago. Someone he almost forgot existed. His mother put her hand on Paddie's shoulder and looked straight at Shogun.

Madigan felt her eyes begin to fill with hot tears. She saw the struggle on Shogun's face as he looked to her. "Bring them back to what?" she whispered.

Shogun's sword began to vibrate. It turned a reddish orange, the color of brilliant fall leaves. Paddie raised his axe to Shogun and nodded. Roland shouted and Shogun could hear his grandfather's battle cry loud and clear. Shogun took the sword by both his hands and the blade began to hum.

"No!" the darkness screamed. It began to claw at the golden net, its long nails breaking through several fibers at a time. Through the holes in the net, dark particles started to seep out and scatter. The outlines of their family members faded away as the shrine began to tremble and deteriorate.

"Now!" Madigan shouted.

The creature scratched frantically at the net. "Idiot! Listen to me!"

Shogun moved towards the darkness now growing in size, the net struggling to keep it contained. His grandfather's battle hymn thumped loudly in his head, along with a thousand other voices crying out for him. He raised up his sword.

"I am listening."

Everything depended on this. Everything.

XXX

THE MYTH OF THE TWO WARRIORS

The tracks looked just as they had left them. Just as they had existed in their memories. Even the afternoon light looked the same as though nothing ever changed. *But things do change,* the trees told Shogun. He walked behind Madigan on the edges of their secret spot, the abandoned tracks they met at time and time again as children. Fall was approaching, the smell of it in the air was unmistakable. Old leaves dying to make way for the new, conceived in the chill of winter. Death then birth, over and over again. And every season the forest would inch a little closer. Soon the tracks would be a forgotten place, known only to the spirits that took their last trip home on the ghost train.

Madigan stopped at the tree line, wrapping her arm around an obliging fir tree. Shogun sat down on a moss-covered log, stretching out his long legs in front of him. They were stiff from spending all day on Madigan's small boat, his boots tucked beneath his seat to make room for the nets full of fish. He watched the sunlight trickle through the branches and settle on her hair, still slightly damp from the sea.

"Don't be disappointed if this doesn't work," he said. "It has been a long time." He hoped for her sake that it did. Seeing his family at the shrine had been enough for him. To finally see his mother's likeness with his own eyes. To see his father and confirm the man he knew as a child had truly existed. To hear his grand-father's battle cry one last time. *But she thinks differently than you*, the trees reminded him with a yawn. Shogun sighed and waved the trees back to sleep. The trees were complacent now, finally at peace with Shogun back in their arms again.

I just want to see them safe, Madigan said to the moon loung-ing above her, just barely visible in the waning afternoon light. The last time that she had seen her family was burned into her mind. It haunted her. She dreamt about them as shattered pieces, trapped beneath the rubble of the fallen shrine, no way to see night or day. Had she left them there? But the moon had nothing to do with that filthy eastern coast, she reminded Madigan with a fluff of her hair. Then she heard the whistle.

"I hear it," she called to Shogun. "I hear it!"

Shogun jumped up and joined her as the wind charged down the tracks, brushing any debris and overgrowth out of the way, nodding to them as it rushed by. Shogun had heard the whistle too, ringing beneath the ground, circulating through the for-est's root systems. The ghost train approached closer and clos-er, the dilapidated tracks rattling in anticipation. In an instant, it was upon them. Car by car passed by at lightning speed. The passengers looked out the windows, catching their last glimpse of the forest before going home.

"I don't see them. Where are they?" Madigan cried out above the rattling of the passing train. It was moving so fast and so packed with passengers, they could have been there and she'd never know. But she had to know. She ran into the tracks, chasing after the last car as it flew past her.

Jacob waited on the steps of the last train car, staring into the passing treetops. He turned as Madigan ran onto the tracks. He smiled as he recognized her, the little girl who felt so very much now grown up. Jacob shook his head as if in awe. Madigan watched as the ghost train disappeared car by car until the last was about to evaporate. Jacob winked and returned inside, closing the door behind him. Madigan inhaled and closed her eyes, remembering that moment forever.

• • •

"Night was fast approaching. The flame in the evening sky had long since disappeared, sinking into the swirling sea beside the shrine. But they could not be afraid of the night. They could not fear the evil that laid within, waiting for them. Or the screams-"

Madigan cleared her throat. Shogun stopped mid-sentence, his balled fist still raised in the air. The firelight made his shadow pump back and forth against the living room wall. He looked down to the wide-eyed children sitting beneath his feet. He lowered his fist and instead took a striking position, holding an invisible axe in his hands.

"When they entered the shrine, the warriors met magic. Real, deep magic, the kind that roams the woods and lives beneath the sea. The evil had taken over every bit of that place, growing enormous and powerful. But the warriors had their two enchanted weapons by their sides."

Shogun paused for effect. His children exchanged glances, waiting for more.

"They could glow," Madigan added. She was standing against the opposite wall, watching and listening.

"Yes," Shogun agreed, pointing in her direction. He closed his eyes, gathering his concentration once again. "Yes, they were magical, enchanted weapons that glowed when danger was near. No one had ever seen anything like it before. And no one ever would again."

"What was the thing in the castle?" his oldest son, Roland, called out. His hands were balled into fists as though ready to strike.

"It was actually a shrine, not a castle. And the creature was an evil spirit with dark eyes. It had captured the ones the warriors loved and it was spreading quickly. Making this world, our world, a very bad place." Shogun paused, watching the children's faces. He saw the growing concern and quickly raised his arms, as though throwing a net through the air.

"So they raised their weapons and challenged the monster, capturing it beneath a net of gold. The creature screamed and tore at the net but could not break through. It was trapped. And it was time to destroy the darkness." Shogun's voice faded into a tense whisper. He straightened and pretended to draw an axe from his back. "It was time to set things right."

Shogun swung, jumping up in the air and landing hard on his booted feet. The children jumped in response to his battle cry.

"The mighty warrior raised his weapon and killed the beast! It faded into nothing, reduced to dust in the wind. Then the shrine began to shake and crumble, as though it had been held together by dark magic the whole time. The two warriors barely escaped alive."

Slowly smoothing out his shirt, Shogun took a deep breath and cleared his throat. His children waited in silence. His storytelling was not as entertaining as his grandfather's had been, he was aware of it. He was still working on the theatrics and knowing when to include dramatic pauses.

"With evil gone and the shrine destroyed, the warriors had won. Their enchanted weapons simply faded away. As did the two warriors, who left to return home victoriously, never to be seen again."

After throwing another log on the fire, Shogun stood in front of the warm flames. He looked up at his axe, mounted on the fireplace mantle. The axe had fallen into a deep sleep, its heartbeat so slow that Shogun only felt it from time to time. Hibernating and recharging but always listening for his call.

Shogun sat down on the floor across from his children. He watched their faces as they discussed and processed the story in hushed voices. He would tell the tale to them again, many times over, always as unnamed warriors. He would expand upon it and add new details, both for him and them. So they could learn and he could remember.

He looked over the heads of his audience to Madigan. His retelling brought her back to those moments now far away. To those actions now retold as a myth by the fireside, the fear and the loss removed from the storyline. She nodded at Shogun. She liked it this way the best.

After the children had gone to bed, Shogun and Madigan turned off all the lights in their tiny house one by one. Their tiny house that was all their own, not of the forest or the sea but somewhere in between. It was their ritual every night, to dismiss the light and look the darkness right in the eye, never finding anything there but moonlight. The moon that night had been listening to Shogun's story from behind the treetops, waiting for any mention of an enchanting celestial object that reigned the night. Gathering her wispy white stole around her, she whisked away for the remainder of the evening. *Maybe next time.*

Roland watched the moon from his bedroom window, his face pressed against the cool glass. His brother and sister were already sleeping soundly beside him on the mattress, their steady breaths as even and calming as the ticking clock. Outside, the evening was preparing for the transition to night. The grasses had flattened and settled against the cool soil, covering the earth like a thick blanket. Roland laid down next to his siblings, allowing his mind to wander back to his father's tale. He imagined the two warriors standing outside the crumbled shrine, battered but victorious. Dawn was approaching, just appearing on the horizon. They walked towards the sun until Roland fell asleep and forever after.

ABOUT THE AUTHOR

Erin Ritch is an indie author, freelance blogger, and the founder of No Wyverns Publishing. After studying at the Vancouver Film School, Erin worked for several years in the film industry before returning to her roots in creative writing. She holds degrees in both Broadcasting and English Literature. A self-professed "chicken mom," she lives with her family on a fledgling farm in rural Oregon.

You can find Erin Ritch online at:

Website	http://ErinRitch.com/
Blog	http://NoWyverns.com/
Twitter	http://Twitter.com/Eritch324/
Facebook	http://Facebook.com/ErinRitchAuthor/

ABOUT THE ILLUSTRATOR

Char Houweling is a professional graphic designer and freelance illustrator. She enjoys drawing, playing video games, riding her bike, and more drawing.

You can view more of her work at:

Website   Http://HouwelingDesign.com/

Facebook   Http://Facebook.com/HouwelingArt/

www.ingramcontent.com/pod-product-compliance
Lightning Source LLC
Chambersburg PA
CBHW051432170626
46809CB00006B/2435